AMBUSH!

Touch the Sky dismounted, threw the horse's bridle, and watched the animal stretch its long neck out to drink from the little streamlet. Everything was a blur, as if his tired eyes saw things underwater. For a moment, just a blessed moment as the horse drank, the tired Cheyenne let his head fall forward and closed his eyes.

When he opened his eyes again, a shock wave of fear slammed into him. He saw Ladislaw had wandered well away from cover to relieve himself, and none of the others had yet noticed him.

Touch the Sky shouted a warning even as Little Horse looked up and also spotted the danger. Both of them started forward with the swiftness of charging cats, closing the distance between them and Ladislaw. Touch the Sky steeled his muscles for the jump, then saw Wolf Who Hunts Smiling stepping from behind a deadfall, an arrow notched in his bow.

Touch the Sky leapt at the same moment Little Horse did. They crashed down onto Ladislaw and toppled him. But they were an eyeblink too late to completely avoid the deadly arrow—as Touch the Sky landed on the doctor, he felt a pain like white-hot fire rip into his back.

14

CHEYENNE

DEATH CAMP
JUDD COLE

LEISURE BOOKS   NEW YORK CITY

A LEISURE BOOK®

June 1995

Published by

Dorchester Publishing Co., Inc.
276 Fifth Avenue
New York, NY 10001

Printed in the United States of America.

Prologue

Though he sat behind few men in council, the tall Cheyenne brave called Touch the Sky faced a future as uncertain as his past.

His original Cheyenne name was lost forever after a bluecoat ambush near the North Platte killed his father and mother. The lone Indian survivor of the bloody battle, the squalling infant was taken back to the Wyoming river-bend settlement of Bighorn Falls near Fort Bates.

He was adopted by John Hanchon and his barren young wife Sarah. Owners of the town's thriving mercantile store, the Hanchons named the boy Matthew and raised him as their own blood. But their love couldn't protect him from the hostility and fear of other white settlers—especially when, at 16, he fell in love with Kristen, daughter of the wealthy and hidebound rancher Hiram Steele.

Steele had Matthew savagely beaten when he caught the Cheyenne youth and Kristen in their secret meeting place. The rancher also warned the boy to stay away from his daughter or face certain death. Frightened for Matthew's life, Kristen lied and told him she never wanted to see him again. Still, Matthew's love for his parents and Kristen kept him in Bighorn Falls.

But Seth Carlson, an arrogant young cavalry lieutenant from Fort Bates, was also in love with Kristen. Either Matthew pulled up stakes for good, he warned, or his parents would lose their lucrative contract with Fort Bates—the lifeblood of their business.

His heart saddened but determined, Matthew Hanchon set out for Cheyenne territory in the up-country of the Powder River. He was immediately captured by braves from Chief Yellow Bear's Northern Cheyenne camp. Declared a spy for the white-skin soldiers, he was tortured and sentenced to die. But just as a young brave named Wolf Who Hunts Smiling was about to gut him, old Arrow Keeper intervened.

The tribe shaman and protector of the sacred medicine arrows, Arrow Keeper had recently experienced an epic vision. His vision foretold that the long-lost son of a great Cheyenne chief would return to his people—and that this youth would lead his people in one last, great victory against their enemies. This youth would be known by the distinctive mark of the warrior, the same birthmark Arrow Keeper spotted buried past the youth's hairline: a mulberry-colored arrowhead.

Keeping all this information to himself to protect the youth from jealous tribal enemies, Arrow Keeper used his influence to spare the prisoner's life. This action infuriated two braves: the cunning Wolf Who Hunts Smiling and his fierce older cousin Black Elk.

Black Elk, the tribe's war leader despite his youth, was jealous of the glances cast at the tall young stranger by Honey Eater, daughter of Chief Yellow Bear. And Wolf Who Hunts Smiling, proudly ambitious, had turned his heart to stone against all whites without exception. This stranger, to him, was only a make-believe Cheyenne who wore white men's shoes, spoke the paleface tongue, and showed his emotions in his face like the woman-hearted white men. He insisted on calling the new arrival Woman Face and White Man Runs Him.

Arrow Keeper, however, buried Matthew's white name forever and named him Touch the Sky. But acceptance did not come with that new name. As he trained to become a warrior, Touch the Sky was humiliated at every turn. And his enemies within the tribe did not cease their relentless campaign to prove he was a spy for the hair faces.

Through sheer determination to find his place,

assisted now and then by the cunning he had learned from white men, Touch the Sky became one of the greatest warriors of the *Shaiyena* nation. His fighting skill and courage won him more and more followers, including the ever loyal braves Little Horse, Two Twists, and Tangle Hair. Under Arrow Keeper's careful eye, Touch the Sky also made great progress in the shamanic arts.

With each victory, however, his enemies managed to turn appearances against him and to suggest that he still carried the white man's stink, which brought the tribe bad luck and scared off the buffalo. Although the entire tribe knew that Touch the Sky and Honey Eater were desperately in love, Honey Eater was forced into a loveless marriage with Black Elk, who chafed in a jealous, murderous wrath, plotting revenge against Touch the Sky.

Arrow Keeper, well into his frosted years, eventually realized he must leave the tribe before Touch the Sky could assume the role of shaman and Arrow Keeper. He departed to build a death wickiup, disappearing and thus leaving the question of his life or death a mystery to the others.

Now Touch the Sky is challenged at every turn by Black Elk and his cousin Wolf Who Hunts Smiling, who argue he cannot be trusted to protect the sacred arrows. Unknown to everyone except the false shaman named Medicine Flute, the ambitious Wolf Who Hunts Smiling is on the brink of taking over the entire Cheyenne nation.

Death Camp

He then plans to join his secret renegade allies in a war of extermination against the white-skin settlers.

Only one man can thwart his bloody scheme: the tall brave named Touch the Sky.

Chapter One

Despite the warm spring sun and the hopeful singing of the meadowlarks, Touch the Sky wore a deep frown. All around him, the Cheyenne summer camp of Chief Gray Thunder's band was joyously alive with preparations for the annual spring dance. Young boys shouted from the common corral, where they were tying bright strips of red flannel to the ponies' tails, readying them for the parades. Merry singing and laughter livened the women's sewing lodge, where the unmarried girls were embroidering dance shawls and sewing the moccasins widely recognized for the best beadwork on the plains. Warriors stood in the doorways of their clan lodges, plaiting new rawhide bridles and clipping bright ceremonial feathers with the distinctive endmarks of their clan or soldier troop.

Another hard winter was behind the tribe. The valleys were no longer locked by ice; soon game would once again be plentiful on the hunting ranges the Cheyenne shared with their Sioux cousins. The rivers and creeks were swollen with crystal-clear snow runoff from the mountains. The new grass was green and lush, already well above the ponies' hocks. Soon the far-flung Cheyenne bands, ten in all, would unite as one for the dance festival.

For all these reasons, hope filled the tribe's collective soul like rain falling on parched earth. But for three sleeps in a row, Touch the Sky had experienced a vision, but it was not just the normal kind of troubling vision. This was an omen that warned of grave danger.

Had the omen concerned him alone, he would hardly have granted it a moment's thought. Truly, danger was the ridge he had lived on since his arrival in camp several winters ago. But this latest omen foretold that he would not be suffering alone. For if this was a true vision, the entire tribe would soon be in a hurting place.

"Brother," a voice said, scattering his thoughts like cottonwood fluff in the wind, "I would ask you a thing."

Touch the Sky glanced up from the mountain-lion skin he was supposed to be adorning with elk's teeth and brightly dyed feathers. He sat cross-legged before the entrance flap of his tipi.

His abode stood on a lone hummock between the nearby Powder River and the rest of the tipis, which were arranged in clan circles.

Although the shaman's lodge, like the chief's, always stood off by itself, Touch the Sky had never lived in a clan circle. His original clan was lost to that elusive thing the white men called history. However, the entrance to his tipi, like that of every Cheyenne tipi on the plains, faced east toward the source of all life—Sister Sun, the day maker. His past may have died in that bluecoat raid 20 winters earlier; but not his need to belong.

Touch the Sky forced his attention back to his visitor. The youth was wiry and somber looking; his hair hung in two braids instead of the loose locks or single braid preferred by most Cheyenne braves.

"Two Twists," Touch the Sky replied, holding his face stern, "when fellow warriors parley in a peace camp, they do not simply spit words at each other like rude white men. Words between friends are important. Sit. Grab a coal from the firepit and light this."

For a moment, surprise glinted in Two Twists' eyes. He was not old enough yet to join a soldier troop. Yet Touch the Sky was offering his best clay pipe, telling the junior warrior that, in Touch the Sky's eyes, he was an equal despite having barely 17 winters behind him.

"Little brother," Touch the Sky said, "why do you gawk like a surprised newborn at a dry dug?

Death Camp

Did you not climb the cliffs of Wendigo Mountain beside me? I mean to be answered, buck! Did you?"

"I did," Two Twists said hastily, a bit of Touch the Sky's proud boasting tone seeping into his own voice.

"When the mad renegade Sis-ki-dee unleashed fifty braves against the five of us, did you cower behind any man?"

"No, shaman, I did not!"

"No, indeed, for you fought like ten men as did your Cheyenne brothers, and we evened the battle for them! I was there; I saw you lift your clout at them to show your contempt. Now I call you a full warrior and my brother, worthy to wear the medicine hat into battle. Now sit and smoke."

Proud elation swelled Two Twists' chest like a deep breath. But only squaws and white men showed their private feelings in their faces for all to see. He held his face impassive as a stone mask. Nor did he thank Touch the Sky. True warriors knew they had earned any praise they got, and thus they owed no man gratitude.

Quietly, content in each other's company, the two braves followed the ancient custom. They smoked to the four directions, at first speaking only of inconsequential matters. Finally Touch the Sky placed the pipe on the ground between them, the signal that serious talk could begin.

"Brother," Two Twists said, "I have just come from a visit at the lodge of the Bow String troopers. The talk went round to past spring dances. Then it touched on a certain topic."

"I am called a shaman by some," Touch the Sky said, "though others call me White Man Runs Him. Still, I know of no magic for cutting sign on the human breast. I would rather a man tell me his thoughts freely than force me to read them like a hidden blood spoor. Speak plain, buck."

"I have known you to make greater medicine than thought reading," Two Twists said. "But I will not make you resort to magic. My question, plainly, is this. May we still pronounce the name of the one who was our shaman before you? I ask this thing because some of the Bow Strings said that he has now crossed over to the Land of Ghosts, that we may never say his name again."

"His name, Cheyenne, is Arrow Keeper. I speak it freely because his fate remains unknown. You may speak it too."

"But he left to build a death wickiup."

Touch the Sky nodded. "So he said, and perhaps he did. But from the moment of birth, puzzled one, we all begin heading toward death. Though Arrow Keeper always speaks truth, sometimes the shaft of his words flies indirectly to the target."

Not all of this answer made clear sense to the youth. But his respect for this tall Cheyenne brave gave Touch the Sky's own words a credence beyond their apparent meaning.

Two Twists watched his friend's nimble fingers deftly work the crude bone awl and buffalo-sinew thread, attaching an elk tooth to the beautiful mountain-lion skin, which had been Arrow Keeper's parting gift to Touch the Sky. The skin marked an important transition in the younger brave's life. For with Arrow Keeper's secret departure from the tribe, Touch the Sky was left his chosen successor. After a sharply divided Council of 40 barely approved him, he became tribal shaman and keeper of the sacred medicine arrows.

Touch the Sky realized full well that both titles were a great honor, so great that many in the tribe refused to grant him the right to them, in their hearts if not openly. But with every honor came grave responsibility. This new omen might perhaps have been sent to Touch the Sky by Arrow Keeper. After all, it was he who had first warned Touch the Sky about the omen, he who had first explained how this particular dream vision foretold great disaster for the tribe as one.

But what, Touch the Sky wondered yet again, was he supposed to do? Seek another vision to learn more? Offer a penance to the high holy ones? As he knew from experience, visions often raised more questions than they answered. At best, they were half-glimpsed shapes in a dense fog. They offered only a frustrating hint, never a clear answer.

"Look here, brother!" a hearty voice called out. "Our ponies grow fatter, the service berries are plump with juice, and these two jays sit with glum winter faces. The cold moons are over, bucks!

Soon our trade goods arrive from the miners; soon we trail the buffalo herds!"

The speaker was the sturdy warrior named Little Horse. He was accompanied by Tangle Hair, a Bow String trooper. Like young Two Twists, both braves had made many mortal enemies within the tribe when they swore their loyalty, their very lives, to Touch the Sky. Little Horse and Touch the Sky had faced death together so often that a strong, easy fellowship bound them.

"Hear the first drums?" Little Horse asked. "Soon the Cheyenne nation will dance, and Touch the Sky will lead us!"

All four braves had recently traded their leggings and knee-length fur moccasins for breechclouts and lighter elkskin moccasins. The tallest of them, Touch the Sky was wide in the shoulders, lean from the hard winter but well muscled for a red man. He had a strong, hawk nose, and he wore his dark hair long and loose. But it was cut high over his eyes to leave his vision clear.

Touch the Sky opened his mouth to reply to his friend. But he bit back his words when yet another familiar pair passed within hearing: Wolf Who Hunts Smiling and his new shadow Medicine Flute.

Tangle Hair spoke in a low voice. "There go two who would eat their own young!"

"Straight words," Little Horse said grimly. "And see how they stare toward us goading."

Wolf Who Hunts Smiling was aptly named.

Even now his sly face was divided by a wolf grin while his swift-as-minnow eyes mocked them across the clearing. Medicine Flute shared his companion's cunning, but not his battle-hardened body. He was slender limbed, with heavy-lidded eyes in a lazy face. As always, he played the monotonous, atonal tune on the human-leg-bone flute for which he was named.

"They look," Touch the Sky said, "but have you noticed a thing, brothers? Wolf Who Hunts Smiling seldom taunts any of us. This new silence is dangerous. His cousin Black Elk mimics him in this. They have finally decided to let deeds speak for them, and they have had a long winter to scheme new treachery."

"As you say," Little Horse said. "More and more within the tribe are beginning to believe Wolf Who Hunts Smiling's bent words about Medicine Flute's big medicine. He goes about playing the big Indian, saying, 'But everyone saw how Medicine Flute first predicted he would burn up a star, then did it before the entire tribe. Let White Man Runs Him match this.'"

Touch the Sky nodded. His lips formed a grim, determined slit as he recalled how that burning star had sent many into hysterics. Most of the tribesmen had never heard of a comet or knew—as Medicine Flute had learned—that white men could predict their passing.

"I have watched Wolf Who Hunts Smiling closely," Touch the Sky said. "His ambition is like a sapling that grows too rapidly and crowds out the growth around it. There was a time when he would hesitate to sully the arrows by shedding Cheyenne blood. That time is long past. Now we four know what no one else in our camp suspects. We have seen proof that he has made private treaties with red enemies of our tribe. His plans are as clear as blood in new snow. He means to kill me and set Medicine Flute up as tribe shaman and arrow keeper. He who controls a tribe's medicine controls its destiny."

Little Horse nodded. "Truly, his ambition is no secret. He preaches to the junior warriors and tells them the red man must launch a war of extermination against the *Mah-ish-ta-shee-da*. He tells them that you are one of their spies, that you work from within to steal our homelands for your white masters."

Little Horse had used the Cheyenne name for whites. It meant yellow eyes, because the first white men the Cheyenne had ever seen were severely jaundiced mountain men.

Even now Wolf Who Hunts Smiling's cunning eyes met Touch the Sky's gaze. They gave Touch the Sky a cold, mocking promise of a hard death soon to come.

"He is reminding you, brother," Tangle Hair said, "that he once walked between you and the campfire. By thus publicly announcing his intention to someday kill you, he is forced to either match word to deed or become a laughingstock."

Death Camp

"He is trouble anytime," Touch the Sky said. "I never take him or his cousin Black Elk lightly. Both would use my guts for tipi ropes. But, brothers, I fear more trouble approaches like rain on top a flood. I have had an omen."

At these words, all three of his companions looked sharply at him. An omen was always important. But when experienced by a brave with the third eye of a shaman, it became crucial.

"What omen, brother?" Little Horse demanded.

"A brief medicine vision was placed over my eyes. I dreamed the entire tribe was riding a high ridge at dawn. And just as Sister Sun rose from her birthplace in the east, a full moon descended in the west. I saw both at once."

All three braves understood the awful significance of this. They stared at him, wordless. Then Touch the Sky heard again the gravelly voice of old Arrow Keeper, drifting back like a memory smell: *Heed any vision in which the sun and a full moon share the sky at once. For such a sign means much pain and suffering ahead for your tribe—perhaps even its destruction.*

Dust hazed the valley of the Little Bighorn, a light golden fog in the slanting rays of late afternoon sun. The river tracked like a looping brown ribbon, winding through lush natural meadows bright with new wildflowers. At the head of a long redrock bluff overlooking the valley, Capt. Seth Carlson sat his big 17-hand cavalry sorrel.

"Yonder comes the bull train," he said to the civilian beside him. "Just like I told you. Twice a year, regular as Big Ben, the miners pack in trade goods for the red Arabs at the Powder River camp. It's a peace price, payment for the right to haul ore out over Cheyenne grantland."

Hiram Steele nodded impatiently. "I've always had a keen grasp of the obvious, Soldier Blue. I once had the contract to supply those goods, remember? Why in the hell do you think I wrote to you and went to all this trouble—for my health?

"That damn Matthew Hanchon and his partner did the hurt dance on me down in Kansas. It was them who got the Cherokees on the warpath against me. By the time the territorial court was done with me, I was lucky I had a pot left to piss in. Now I plan to give as good as I got. And if I can't get Hanchon direct, I'll get him through his tribe."

Steele's flint-gray eyes squinted out from a big, angular face. He sat a dark cream stallion with a black mane and tail. Satisfaction oozed from the hard creases of his face as he watched the long column of pack animals below. Their panniers and pack saddles were filled with badly needed contract goods for the Cheyennes: powder and lead, flour, meat, coffee, sugar, tobacco, cloth, and blankets.

Indians were highly partial to blankets, Steele told himself again. His lips eased back from his teeth in a smile. He tugged one rein until his horse turned around. Well back from the two men, a lone Crow Indian held the lead line of a pack-horse. It was piled high with new wool blankets, bright red ones, like the old Hudson's Bay blankets that Indians prized.

"That Crow know what he's handling?" Steele said.

Carlson nodded. "He got the vaccine in time to survive. Once you've had the disease, you can't catch it again. He's the one who wrapped the dead bodies in the blankets."

"You're sure this will do it?"

Again Carlson nodded. "We lost plenty of men at Fort Bates from mountain fever until Washington finally sent out the vaccine," he said. "It's rough. You get the ague and the shakes real bad. Then you just burn and burn with fever till you dehydrate. It took out an entire Blackfoot village up north."

Steele met the younger man's eyes. "You getting snow in your boots? Maybe you've been listening to the Indian-loving Quakers?"

Carlson snorted. "Stuff! I got as much right as you to hate Hanchon, maybe more. He's only cost you money. He's cost me promotions and your daughter."

Steele said nothing. It was true that Kristen had once been in love with the Cheyenne—a source of shame that Steele would never live down. However, he also knew that Carlson was wrong about one thing. Kristen had never been the officer's girl and never would be. But let Carlson think what he wanted to because he too longed to kill Hanchon with a desire as powerful as hell thirst. Such an ally was useful.

"You say you know the lead bull whacker?" Steele said.

"Know him real good. Name's Orrick. He hangs out at the sutler's store at the fort."

"You think he can be persuaded?"

Carlson laughed, strong white teeth flashing from a weathered face. "Can he be persuaded? Would a cow lick Lot's wife? Show him that high-grade you got in your saddlebag, he'll nail his colors to our mast. He'll go blind long enough for us to slip those blankets into the load."

Steele nodded and his eyes puckered in satisfaction. He turned again and nodded at the Crow. Then all three men chucked up their horses, leading their load of death down into the valley.

Chapter Two

"Aunt?"

Honey Eater was busy sewing an embroidered hem on her little niece's calico dress. Without glancing up, she said, "Yes? What is it, little one?"

Laughing Brook watched her favorite aunt closely. She was glad that mean Uncle Black Elk was not here. Now she could spend precious time alone with Honey Eater. The child agreed with the general camp opinion that Honey Eater was the prettiest woman in Gray Thunder's tribe, and no Cheyenne tribe was ever short of beauties.

"Why did all the people shout and cheer when True Brave flashed mirror signals from Bald Mountain?"

"Because his signals meant welcome news. Our trade goods are coming."

"Trade goods?" Laughing Brook, like more and more young girls in camp, had taken to braiding white columbine petals in her long hair, copying Honey Eater.

"Yes, trade goods," Honey Eater said. "This calico cloth we used to make your pretty festival dress. The sugar you like to stir in your yarrow tea. Do you like the crisp meat that sizzles and curls, the fragrant meat called bacon?"

Laughing Brook nodded solemnly. "I like it better than buffalo."

"Well, then, bacon, too, arrives soon with our goods. Child, stop fidgeting so. I'll be done soon!"

"But, Aunt? Who sends these fine presents?"

"They are not presents, little one. They are paid to us by the paleface miners."

"But why? Palefaces hate us. They kill us and hurt our ponies."

"Yes," Honey Eater said with patient sadness, "many do, but not all of them. Some try to speak one way to the Indian, to treat us as their friends. The miner's chief Caleb Riley is a man of honor. He promised that we would share their wealth with them so long as they use our land."

Late morning sunlight slanted through the huge tipi's smokehole. It highlighted the flawless topaz skin of both aunt and niece.

"Aunt?" Laughing Brook's eyes cut shyly away. "Medicine Flute has been speaking about the palefaces. He says they are all our enemies. He said that—"

Death Camp

"He said what, little one?"

"He said that Touch the Sky grew up among white skins. He said Touch the Sky carries the stink that scares off the buffalo herds. He said that Touch the Sky leaves messages hidden in trees for bluecoats, that he is our enemy."

Sparks snapped in Honey Eater's dark almond-shaped eyes. She ignored her work, taking the girl's frail shoulders in her slim, strong hands.

"Child, have ears for your aunt, who loves you as much as she loves life itself. I am about to speak words you must place close to your heart forever. Do you understand?"

Solemnly, Laughing Brook nodded, and Honey Eater said, "Little one, we Cheyenne do indeed have many enemies. And it is true that Touch the Sky has friends among the white skins who raised him. But never believe that Touch the Sky is your enemy. This Medicine Flute, who blows hollow notes from a grisly bone—not once has this one ever shouted the war cry in defense of his tribe.

"But Touch the Sky? All of us—every woman, child, and grandparent in this camp—are alive today because of his bravery and suffering. Do you remember the buffalo hunt to the south when Kiowas and Comanches stole us?"

"Yes, we were hungry, and they hurt us."

"They did, child. But Touch the Sky saved us. These goods about to arrive—with only the help of his brave friend Little Horse, Touch the Sky earned them for us. At great risk, he helped the white skins build their road for the iron horse."

"Does Touch the Sky make you smile inside?" Laughing Brook asked with the candid curiosity of youth.

Honey Eater swallowed audibly. Her throat swelled shut so all she could do was nod.

Laughing Brook looked confused. "But you are married to Uncle Black Elk?"

Again Honey Eater nodded, her face a study in misery. She glanced around her comfortable home and realized it was really two lodges, and the center pole had become the boundary line. She was married to a brave whom once she had respected, but had come to loathe with all her being. His jealous and angry decision to quit lying with her was the only welcome thing he ever did for her. His belligerent accusations had turned to a quiet, dangerous hatred.

Laughing Brook was quiet for a long time, thinking. Then she sighed, unable to comprehend the mysterious ways of adults. Suddenly, from outside, came the voice of the excited camp crier as he rode up and down the village paths: "The pack train is in sight! The pack train is in sight! Soon our goods arrive!"

Letting loose an exclamation of joy, Laughing Brook spun around and ran outside. Honey Eater knew that she too should feel elation. The winter had been long and hard, and most in the tribe had spent it huddled over their firepits. The arrival of this pack train meant welcome diversion from many moons of monotony and suffering.

So why, she wondered, did it feel like a cold fist of ice had replaced her stomach?

Touch the Sky hoped to catch a glimpse of Honey Eater in all the confusion and excitement of the bull train's arrival. But only young Laughing Brook emerged from Honey Eater's tipi. The girl's long braid streamed out behind her as she raced across the central clearing to join Chief Gray Thunder and the throng in front of the council lodge.

The pack animals had been formed up in a circle for the initial inspection and unloading. River of Winds, one of the most trusted braves in camp, was in charge of this duty, assisted by several of his fellow Bow String troopers. The Bow String troopers were the most popular soldiers because of their leader Spotted Tail's firm belief that negotiation was the best way to solve conflicts.

River of Winds moved from animal to animal, checking each load, then nodding his approval to the lead bull whacker. Once before, as the result of Hiram Steele's duplicity, cleverly disguised shoddy goods had been delivered. So River of Winds meticulously inspected each load, looking for flat stones in the slabs of bacon, making sure the salt pork was not marked condemned for troop use. Patiently, the Bow Strings kept the excited people back so the unloading could proceed.

"Brother," Little Horse said close to Touch the

Sky's ear, "look. Wolf Who Hunts Smiling and Black Elk call Caleb Riley's miners your white masters. They named you White Man Runs Him after you helped them. They swore to never touch these goods. Now see how they are poised to make the first grab! It's every Indian for himself, and the Wendigo take the hindmost."

Touch the Sky glanced toward the little stand of willows, where the Bull Whips had gathered. Even as his attention sought them out, Black Elk looked over at him. Like angry stags about to clash over territory, they aggressively held the stare, a long measure of their mutual contempt and hatred.

Black Elk had been the tribe's war leader for as long as Touch the Sky could remember, and a good choice, at that. When the war cry sounded, there was no soft place left in Black Elk's breast, nor could fear touch him. And at first, though as hard as white man's tempered steel, he had tried to be fair to Touch the Sky.

But by now all the people knew about the great love between Touch the Sky and Honey Eater, they knew that she would never have accepted Black Elk's bride price if she had not believed, with all her heart, that Touch the Sky had chosen a white woman over her and deserted the tribe forever. Too late, she found out she was mistaken.

"Yes," Touch the Sky finally replied, still watching Black Elk, "they will take more than their share, meantime demanding the blood of all white men."

"From the look of him, brother," Little Horse said, "Black Elk is keen for Cheyenne blood—yours."

The Bull Whips forced their way closer through the crowd, cracking their highly feared knotted-thong whips to make room. Touch the Sky could clearly see Black Elk with his dark scowl and his fierce eyes like black agates. Most noticeable, however, was the dead flap of his left ear. It had been severed in battle by a bluecoat saber. After Black Elk killed the soldier, he had sewn his own ear back on with buckskin thread. It hung there lopsided, as wrinkled and dry as overtanned leather.

The inspection was finally over. The Bow Strings were heaping the goods for distribution by clans. The white bull whackers were recruiting their animals for the long ride out.

Abruptly, Touch the Sky felt a cool insect prickle moving up his spine, lifting the fine hairs on the back of his neck. He sensed danger the way a burro senses a snake before seeing it. By now he was long familiar with the subtle warnings of his shaman sense.

"What is it, Cheyenne?" Little Horse demanded. He watched storm clouds gather on his friend's brow. But Touch the Sky said nothing. His eyes had locked with those of the lead bullwhacker.

The man was typical of his companions in this

trade—string bean thin, tough as sinew, his filthy hair tied in a heavy knot on the back of his neck. An 18-inch Bowie protruded from his sash, as did a cap-and-ball dragoon pistol. All the men were so filthy that Touch the Sky could see fleas leaping from them.

However, close calls in the past had taught the men some manners with the Indians. They wisely removed the scalps from their sashes before arriving, and they made sure to give the peace sign when riding into camp. Cheyennes were not cold-blooded, and few would fire without being attacked first. But if whites offended the Cheyenne chief or the wrong warrior, they might leave camp minus their topknots.

But Touch the Sky read none of this in the bull whacker's look. It wasn't fear he read there. Instead, oddly enough, he read a quick hint of furtive guilt. The face of a man about to do something he hadn't quite accepted in his heart. But what? This was a hard man who would not easily feel the prick of conscience.

However, before Touch the Sky could puzzle it out further, the white skin turned away, and the men were kneeling to untie the animals' hobbles, preparing to ride out.

"Brother," Little Horse said again, "what have you felt or seen?"

Touch the Sky shook his head. He watched the clan headmen lining up for their distribution of goods. "Something," he replied miserably.

Death Camp

"Enough to worry, too little to act. But I suspect we will have our answer soon enough, and we will be sorry to have it."

Touch the Sky was right: Trouble was seldom bashful about announcing itself. After all, he was poised for its arrival, fully warned by his medicine dream and his premonition when the goods were unloaded. Even so, when the enemy came, it was as unexpected as it was devastating. And it was an enemy that rendered a warrior's skill useless.

After the distribution of the goods, one sleep passed without incident. The first far-flung bands of the Northern Cheyenne were due to arrive at any time for the spring dance. Anticipation of their arrival, plus the holiday mood caused by the pack train's windfall, left Gray Thunder's camp in high spirits.

The clan and lodge fires shot orange spear tips into the air all night long. Younger braves gambled on foot and pony races. Older braves sneaked behind their lodges to drink weak corn beer and recite their coups to any who cared to listen. The women hovered near the cooking pits to roast elk and antelope meat for the dance feast, meantime exclaiming over the fine quality of the cloth sent by the miners. The children ran wild everywhere, playing at taking scalps and counting coups. Stirred up by all the unusual activity, the camp dogs howled and barked as if moon crazy.

Then, on the second morning after the pack

train departed, a woman's sudden scream of grief and terror split the predawn stillness. In a heartbeat, his warrior's body responding even before his mind woke up, Touch the Sky was out of his robes and groping for his Sharps percussion rifle. Eyes still clogged with the cobwebs of slumber, he stumbled out of his tipi into the grainy chill.

Other braves also assumed the camp was under attack. Many rushed out of their tipis still naked. Whoever the invaders, it was the warriors' first responsibility to form a line of defense behind which the women, children, and elders could escape by hidden trails. But there was no attack. Instead, there was a flurry of activity around one of the tipis of the Broken Lance Clan.

"What has happened, brother?" Little Horse called out, meeting up with Touch the Sky in the gathering throng.

Touch the Sky shook his head. A horrible feeling of doom had settled deep into his bones. They watched young Two Twists, who had reached the tipi before most of the others. He turned and fought his way through the curious people, anxious to reach his friends.

Even limited to the light of a full moon and a few dying camp fires, Touch the Sky could see that Two Twists' face was urgent with worry.

"What passes?" Little Horse demanded. Even as he spoke, several old grandmothers began keening in grief. The cry was taken up by others.

"The little one who was Dancing Woman's baby

has gone under! And brothers, three more children are dying!"

This terrible news struck the two braves with the force of bluecoat canister shot. Cheyennes, like Apaches, valued their children over all else. Even the stern warriors cried openly at the funeral scaffold of a child. To Cheyennes, every adult in camp was the parent of every child.

"Gone under?" Touch the Sky said woodenly. "But how? From what?"

It cost Two Twists a physical effort to speak the dreaded words. "From mountain fever," he replied, and Touch the Sky felt his face drain cold.

Chapter Three

Mountain fever! The words struck as much fear in Touch the Sky as might the sentry's wolf howl of alarm. How many Indian camps had been wiped out or nearly destroyed by this mysterious and dreaded disease? Touch the Sky knew that a Pawnee attack would have been a kindness compared to this.

Nor could there be any mistaking the disease. It always ravaged children more quickly than it did adults. It literally burned the life out of them, killing them rapidly from total dehydration—as Dancing Woman's child had died, as more were dying even now.

The urgency of the situation meant they could not wait for the usual Council of 40. Chief Gray Thunder, through the camp crier, announced a council of the warriors to take place as soon as emergency measures could be taken for dealing with the crisis.

Strips of black cloth were tied to the tipis where infections had broken out. A few elders and women began constructing a hasty pest lodge. The infected would be moved in together and tended by a few Cheyennes who had beaten incredible odds and survived the illness, thus becoming immune.

How many more would be struck down? Touch the Sky saw that very question in the eyes of everyone he met. Even as the pest lodge took shape, additional chilling news flew through camp. The first adult was sick, a grandfather in the Rattlesnake Clan. Touch the Sky's eyes flew constantly to Black Elk's tipi, hoping for a reassuring glimpse at Honey Eater.

"Brother," Little Horse said, "the talk grows ugly over near the Bull Whip lodge. Black Elk and Wolf Who Hunts Smiling are working their brothers up to a frenzy against you. They say the white freighters brought this disease. They say that it was deliberate and that it could never have happened if you did not gnaw the bones thrown to you by palefaces. I fear they have some plan afoot and mean to make your life a hurting place at the council."

"No doubt they do, buck. When have they ever missed a chance to fan the fires against me? Let them. Here I stand, a living man despite all their efforts. The first one of them foolish enough to bridge the gap will be dead before he hits the ground."

Although his boast was sincere enough, Touch the Sky spoke it absently. He was still thinking about Little Horse's words and glancing uneasily at Black Elk's tipi, wondering and fearing. He wished with all his might that Arrow Keeper were still there; his wisdom was always as reassuring as the lee of a mesa in a windstorm.

"I fear they are right about one thing," Touch the Sky said, forcing his eyes back to Little Horse. "It was the freighters who brought the disease to us."

Little Horse nodded glumly. "It is no fault of yours, warrior. But I fear you have truth firmly by the tail. If so, then I too share the blame. For did I not help you sight the path through for the iron horse?"

"Never mind blame. Though the cause may be secret, the effect is known. But it was the freighters."

"Them," Little Horse said, "or something they left has this bad medicine clinging to it."

Others too had come to this conclusion. As the day's new sun tracked higher across the sky, more and more in the tribe fell ill. And finally, the mystery was explained as the one telltale pattern emerged clearly. The afflicted Cheyennes shared one fact in common: They had worn or slept in one of the recently delivered blankets.

A survivor of an earlier clash with the disease

was sent round to gather every single blanket that had been distributed. Huge clouds of black smoke billowed into the sky as the wool blankets were burned in the camp clearing. The moment Touch the Sky learned of this, he hurried to River of Winds' tipi.

His agitation was great. Not every clan received blankets from each consignment of goods. Had Honey Eater or Black Elk acquired one this time? River of Winds had distributed the goods; he would know which clans had received them. Touch the Sky suddenly pulled up short when he saw black flannel tied to the elkskin entrance flap of River of Winds' tipi.

Of course the brave would be sick, Touch the Sky realized. Had River of Winds not touched all the goods, blankets included? The pest lodge was not yet completed, so River of Winds should still be inside alone, since his own wife and child had been killed one winter earlier by the yellow vomit.

"River of Winds? It is Touch the Sky. Can you hear me, brother?"

"I hear you," came the weak reply from inside. "But come no closer unless you are eager to feed the worms."

Touch the Sky winced. The brave's voice was already drawn tight with pain and suffering. "Brother, I am sorry for your illness. Indeed, it comes upon the heels of hard fortune for you. But be strong. You and the other sick ones are neither forgotten nor gone from this life. We are Cheyennes. We take care of our own. Soon we will move you to the pest lodge, and the cure songs will be sung over you night and day. Only will you tell me a thing"

"As for cure songs, tell the old women to sing away. I do not wish to die alone in silence. For, brother, I am gone, and so are the others. Better to build our scaffolds and sew us new moccasins for this final journey. But speak. What thing would you have me tell you?"

Again Touch the Sky's troubled brow wrinkled. The pain must be great, for River of Winds was not given to easy pessimism. "Were blankets distributed to the Panthers or the Antelope?"

There was a long excruciating silence while Touch the Sky nerved himself for bad news.

"Neither clan received blankets this time," River of Winds finally answered. And because he understood why Touch the Sky had asked, he added, "I envy you this love, for now that I am dying nothing else matters but death. Still, rest easy on one score at least. Unless she becomes careless, Honey Eater will survive."

A heavy stone was lifted from Touch the Sky's chest by River of Winds' words. But as his fear for Honey Eater lessened, his concern for the afflicted increased.

The pest lodge—a large structure made from bent saplings covered with hides—was completed. Though the danger of infection was great,

Touch the Sky knew he must risk a visit. If the people could not count on the strength of their shaman, what was left to them? Had Arrow Keeper ever cowered in his tipi when smallpox or the red-speckled cough ravaged the camp?

The emergency council was set to begin soon. Touch the Sky would have just enough time to sing a brief prayer to bless the new lodge with good medicine.

Solemnly he prepared. First he visited the sweat lodge to meditate while cleansing his pores in hot steam. After drying himself with clumps of sage, he donned his best beaded leggings, leather shirt, and crow-feather warbonnet. Then, leaving all his weapons in his tipi, he walked to the pest lodge.

Worried loved ones formed a ring around the lodge. A second baby had died, and mourning cries filled the camp. Several of the people cleared a path as Touch the Sky headed for the entrance. Some of them looked grateful for the visit. Several others, influenced by Wolf Who Hunts Smiling and the clever shaman Medicine Flute, shot resentful glances at him.

As Touch the Sky's hand gripped the hide flap, he again felt a warning moving like a cool feather along the bumps of his spine. He threw back the flap. Immediately the fragrant smoke of sweetgrass and dogwood incense wafted into his nostrils. It was dim within, the air strident with the sound of painful and labored breathing. Above the sweet tang of the incense hung the musty stench of serious illness. Somewhere a child whimpered.

Black Elk and Wolf Who Hunts Smiling never showed pity in their faces. But Touch the Sky knew that compassion, when it was due, was the mark of a true warrior. His deep concern for these innocent sufferers who shared his blood made him vow to face the Wendigo himself, if he must, to save them. And again he silently thanked Maiyun that Honey Eater had been spared. Deep in his heart of hearts he knew, if she should die before he did, he would not want to live.

The sick Cheyennes—including men, women, and children—were scattered about on heaps of robes. Touch the Sky spotted Sharp Nosed Woman, Honey Eater's aunt and a rare survivor of mountain fever, moving from one victim to the next. She held a gourd filled with cool water to the patients' dry lips and patted their burning faces with wet cloths. The moment she spotted Touch the Sky, her jaw fell slack. She shot him a beseeching look, as if she were suffering from some terrible guilt.

"Touch the Sky, can you forgive me? I am truly sorry. Indeed, if we lose her, my grief will cry out to heaven alongside yours. But how could I have known? How?"

Touch the Sky shook his head, baffled. "Forgive you? Sharp Nosed Woman, if a better Cheyenne woman than you lives in our camp, I have yet to meet her. Speak words I can carry off in my sash.

If we lose whom? How could you have known what?"

It was her turn to frown in puzzlement. "Two Twists did not tell you?"

"Tell me what, sister?"

"He did not tell you how I received one of the new blankets? How I traded it for a shawl she embroidered?"

But suddenly Touch the Sky heard nothing else. His world was spinning round like a leaf trapped in a whirling dervish. He had just spotted the young woman lying near the back wall of the pest lodge—or rather he spotted the soft white blur of the columbine petals braided through Honey Eater's hair.

"The filthy dogs who brought this sickness were lured to our camp by White Man Runs Him! It was he who helped the white skins build their iron road over our land. It was he who drank devil water with them at the trading post, he who deserted his tribe to fight for whites. Will a fish leave the river and live in the trees with birds? He is a pretend Cheyenne, sent among us by bluecoats to work their malevolent plans from within!"

Rarely had the fiery-tempered Wolf Who Hunts Smiling been in better speaking form. At his words, Black Elk's fist shot into the air and a shout of support exploded throughout the council lodge.

"This White Man Runs Him," Wolf Who Hunts Smiling said, "has far more in his parfleche than our doting elders suspect. He wears two faces, and he wears them well. I say again he is involved in a scheme to take our hunting ranges! He will help to kill us off, then share the profits with his soldier brothers."

But before the eloquent speaker could whip himself to an even higher pitch, Little Horse was on his feet. Normally, Touch the Sky could hold his own with any man in council. But Little Horse knew his friend was devastated.

"Listen to this wily wolf! Lies and treachery come so naturally to him that it is like breathing. Ask him about his private treaties with our enemies Sis-ki-dee and Big Tree. And still he rails against Caleb Riley and his miners. Yet see that twine-handled knife in his sheath? The fat tobacco pouch on his sash? I saw him drinking coffee this morning, cramming his greedy and lying face with hot bacon—he who mourns so for our sick and dying. He speaks from both sides of his mouth, and neither side speaks straight."

"They cannot," Tangle Hair said, "for he is too busy chewing white man's bacon."

At this remark, many Bow String troopers roared with laughter. Even Gray Thunder grinned in spite of himself. Never, Touch the Sky thought through his numbness, had he seen the council so sharply divided. Indeed, despite this momentary levity, this new tragedy was pushing the tribe to the brink of internal war. Chief Gray Thunder seemed to have aged ten winters in the last two sleeps. The tribe was pulling two ways despite his best efforts to keep them unified as one people.

Gray Thunder folded his arms until the lodge had quieted again. "Cheyenne people, have ears. No more jokes while our loved ones lie dying! More and more are falling ill. I have been forced to send word bringers out to warn our fellow *Shaiyenas* they must not enter our camp. The spring dance cannot be held. We all know that Wolf Who Hunts Smiling and Touch the Sky would gladly feed each other's liver to the dogs. This is no time for them to strut and make the he-bear talk. Our loved ones come first."

Touch the Sky's voice joined the chorus of approval for these words. Only one image dominated his troubled mind: Honey Eater lying in that pest lodge, her life ebbing away.

"Therefore," Gray Thunder said, "I will let both sides state their plan. No matter how some may feel, Touch the Sky is our official shaman. Arrow Keeper selected him, and no man on the entire plains has greater wisdom or stronger medicine than Arrow Keeper. Therefore, Touch the Sky will speak first."

The council lodge was as quiet as a sleeping camp at dawn. Touch the Sky rose. He saw Black Elk and Wolf Who Hunts Smiling glowering at him. Touch the Sky held his face impassive.

"My council will not be well received. But like our chief, I care not for brave talk and scowls, only to save our people."

"To save one of them," Black Elk said, "for he is keen to rut on her! The rest he does not value at a gnat's breath."

"This dead-eared braggart says I do not value our people. Yet look at his shame! His good wife lies dying; two children have just crossed over. Has grief moved him to compassion or the decency to work calmly with his tribe to fight this new trouble? No! He does dirt on a good woman and seizes her tragedy as one more reason to shed tribal blood and sully our sacred arrows!"

Gray Thunder had dreaded this turn of events. Violence lay thick in the air, and rage blazed in Black Elk's face. Several of the Bull Whips were forced to restrain him.

"Just what does White Man Runs Him have in mind?" Wolf Who Hunts Smiling demanded scornfully. "More cooperation with bluecoats?"

"Yes," Touch the Sky said without hesitation. His defiant answer hung in the air like the echo of a rifle shot. Even his friends looked surprised. "Our goal is to save the people. The peace road is the quickest route to that goal. The only ones who possess the magic called vaccine are the blue-bloused soldiers at Fort Bates. They have medicine men called doctors and know how to shoot this vaccine into the sick ones. I speak their tongue. I will approach them under a truce flag."

"No!" Wolf Who Hunts Smiling leapt to his feet. "This plan has the white man's stink all over it! I still say it was white soldiers who caused this disease to be among us, and perhaps this woman-faced pretend Cheyenne has helped them. Now he means to pretend to seek help from them, thus giving this mountain fever time to kill us off. We must take hostages and force white skins to help us!"

Pandemonium broke out when the wily young brave quit speaking. Only after he was forced to shout could Gray Thunder quiet the others enough to speak. Known for his even temper, he spoke with impatience straining his voice.

"Brothers! Will we shed blood at our very council, as do the barbaric Comanches? Enough of this bitter fighting. I am weary from it. The headmen will vote with their stones. White stones back Touch the Sky; black stones favor Wolf Who Hunts Smiling's plan. Whatever the stones decide will be final."

Each voting headman carried two stones in his parfleche: a white moonstone and a black agate. Gray Thunder started passing round the chamois pouch used for voting. Keeping his choice hidden in his hand, each headman slipped a stone inside.

As the pouch made its rounds, Touch the Sky's agitation was deep. Finally, the pouch was passed back to Gray Thunder, and he was on the verge of spilling the stones out onto the robes beneath him.

But now Touch the Sky reminded himself that Honey Eater was dying! Abruptly, agonizingly trapped between his love for Honey Eater and his duty to the Cheyenne way, Touch the Sky rebelled.

He seized the pouch from Gray Thunder before the stones could be spilled out. Gray Thunder's jaw slacked open in surprise.

"I am following only one plan," Touch the Sky announced boldly. "My own. Maiyun have mercy on any brave who attempts to stop me."

"This is open treason!" Wolf Who Hunts Smiling shouted. In a blink he was on his feet again, his knife in his hand. Black Elk and several other Bull Whips rose up with him. "Now he dies!"

But just as quickly, Little Horse, Tangle Hair, and Two Twists formed a ring around their leader. They too had weapons in hand.

"Come, then," Little Horse said softly, "and let the battle be bloody or nothing else!"

But no one moved. No ten braves in the tribe could have touched the tall shaman now—not through that ring of fighting Cheyennes. Bloodshed was barely avoided for the moment.

Gray Thunder shook his head in disgust. "Only look on this spectacle of shame. Our tribe's shaman makes a mockery of the headmen's vote. Our tribe's war leader and his cousin stand ready to kill a fellow Cheyenne in front of their peace chief. All this while death ravages our camp. I have lived too long to see a chief reduced to a squaw by his own people."

Gray Thunder rose, signifying that the council was over. "I am ashamed of these proceedings. I will not light the common pipe again and touch it with my lips, for I cannot sanction these events."

Death Camp

He stared at Touch the Sky. "But I confess, buck, I voted for your plan and still back it. You have today disgraced the Cheyenne laws. I will consider your wrongdoing redeemed, however, if you bring this doctor and magic vaccine back in time to help our people."

Black Elk spoke next. "They will be brought back, indeed." His murderous stare knifed into Touch the Sky. "I am this tribe's war leader, and I decide our plan of battle—not even Gray Thunder can override me. And it is my wife who lies dying, not Woman Face's. So I spit his words back into his face. Maiyun have mercy on any brave who attempts to stop me."

Chapter Four

"We'll bivouac here for the night," Capt. Seth Carlson told his platoon sergeant. "Looks like rain later, so tell the men to snap their shelter halves together before they bed down. Full bandoliers and every swinging dick is to have a light-marching pack ready at all times. If we engage these hostiles, we'll be covering plenty of landscape."

"That we will, sir," Sgt. Nolan Reece said, "assuming you mean Injin hostiles. I've never met the Injun yet who liked to fort up for a battle. The sneaking red devils fight from horseback and skirmish from behind rocks."

The two soldiers sat their mounts in the long shadow of a huge granite headland known as Lookout Bluff. The Shoshone River lay out of sight to the north, the rim of its shallow valley marked by the occasional clump of wind-twisted cottonwoods. Off and on for 20 years, since establishing the lonely remount post of Fort Bates in the southeast Wyoming Territory, the army had used this spot as an observation post and mirror station. Lookout Bluff commanded an impressive view of the territory's vulnerable northern approach, which was ranged by several hostile tribes and especially prone to raiding by the fierce Sioux and their equally fierce Cheyenne cousins. Behind the two soldiers, a 40-man platoon of cavalry and dragoon sharpshooters held double columns at wide intervals.

"Set up picket outposts," Carlson said. "Two-hour watches. We'll graze the horses farther out while it's still light, then bring them close to camp at dark."

"Yes, sir." Reece glanced discreetly away, out over the vast brown onsweep of short-grass prairie to the north. Any Indians heading south toward the fort or Bighorn Falls would have to cross it. "I understand, sir, that we're currently at peace with all the tribes in this sector and that we have standing orders to avoid them completely except for defensive actions if attacked."

He spoke casually, keeping any note of disapproval out of his tone. Reece liked duty under his new company commander. For like him, Carlson hated Indians with a passion that bordered on the fanatical. Sgt. Reece had once led a scouting patrol on a private mission to sack an Apache camp down in Ojo Caliente while their men were off hunting. But he didn't understand then how fiercely Indian women and children would fight for their homes. A stone-headed war club had shattered his right knee and left him limping badly for life.

Carlson knew his platoon sergeant was only hinting for information, not rebelling at this mysterious new training exercise.

"Except for defensive actions if attacked," Carlson repeated. "Law-abiding soldiers have a right to defend themselves. Don't you agree, Sergeant?"

"Speak the truth and shame the devil, sir."

"And let's just say the head of one of the Indians who attack us happened to be worth two thousand dollars to a certain merchant I happen to know. Now, if the Indians were attacking us anyway, killing him would only sweeten the victory a little."

"That it would, sir. It most certainly would, for a fact."

"Personally, I'd be more than willing to share that two thousand dollars with a fellow soldier, especially if he was to use his influence with the men and persuade them not to contradict our field reports back in garrison."

Reece grinned. Broken teeth flashed under a long teamster's mustache. "Sir, my hand to God, they're good lads all. Fine soldiers who 'preciate a pint of cool beer or a glass of Knockum Stiff. You point 'em, Cap'n. I'll make sure they peddle lead to the right red customers."

Carlson nodded. Most of his big bluff face lay in shadow under the snap brim of his officer's hat.

"You fairly certain, are you, sir, that the hostiles you have in mind will be riding this way?"

Carlson thought about that question. Only a miracle could have protected Matthew Hanchon's tribe from infection. With luck, the tall, trouble-making buck would catch the disease and die. If not, he would surely take it on himself to approach Fort Bates for help. Probably knew about the vaccine and the contract surgeons the fort kept around.

Carlson also thought about all the damn good reasons he had for sending this red son across the Great Divide. Chief among many that rankled at him was that humiliating business with Hiram Steele's daughter Kristen. It still made Carlson blush pink clear to his ear lobes to realize that she had preferred a full-blooded Cheyenne buck over him, a white man. She chose to kiss the lips of a filthy, gut-eating savage rather than those of a graduate of West Point, the scion of a Virginia senator!

"If I know this buck like I think I do," Carlson finally replied, "he'll be riding this way. But I'll warn you right now: Killing him will be a rough piece of work."

Reece reached down to massage his sore right knee. Each winter it stiffened up bad and made walking or mounting a horse harder and harder.

Soon the army would have to cashier his lame carcass, and Reece was fit for no other calling.

"Two thousand dollars?" he said.

Carlson nodded. "In double eagle gold pieces."

Reece flashed his broken teeth again, glancing back down the double columns. "Rough work is the only kind I know, sir," he finally replied. "You know what they say about Injuns. 'Injuns are only nits, but nits make lice.' I say let's kill some nits."

Touch the Sky's worst enemy was a familiar one: time. He did not know exactly how long Honey Eater or the rest had left before it would be too late for the white man's medicine—assuming he ever got any. Certainly not long. Perhaps the strongest of them might last a few sleeps. Riding hard and eating on horseback, they could reach Fort Bates in one-and-a-half sleeps. So even if everything went right, help could not be had in less than three days. And truly, Touch the Sky asked himself, when had everything ever gone right?

"Brother," Little Horse said soon after the nearly fatal council meeting, "I know who is riding with Black Elk. I saw them cutting their ponies out of the common corral. Not surprisingly, the white-livered Medicine Flute will remain in camp. He is to work medicine over our sick."

"Add his medicine to your empty quiver," Tangle Hair said, "and you are out of arrows."

"Straight enough," Little Horse said. He aimed

a searching glance at Touch the Sky. "But there are some whose medicine is real and strong. I only wonder why do they not use their powers more often during trouble?"

"Perhaps the medicine uses the man," Touch the Sky said evasively, "and picks the occasion. A shaman who could use magic at his whim would not be a man but a god. He must impress the high holy ones first and prove that he is worthy of help."

The same three comrades who protected Touch the Sky in council were preparing to ride out with him. All four braves had joined the rest of the adult males in cropping short their hair in sympathy for their dead. It was tacitly agreed among them that Touch the Sky was their leader in any crisis. Once they had wondered why the young buck did not join a warrior society—the Bow Strings, in particular, since he admired them and their leader Spotted Tail. But now they understood Touch the Sky was marked out for a far greater destiny—destiny in which he would lead his own vast faction. He was meant to lead, not join.

"Medicine Flute is staying back," Little Horse said. "Riding with Black Elk are Wolf Who Hunts Smiling, the Bull Whip named Stone Mountain, and Swift Canoe, who has recently been initiated as a Bull Whip."

"Four warriors who equal ten," Touch the Sky said glumly. "Swift Canoe is a feather brain, but I have seen even that one cleave a Pawnee in half."

As he finished rigging his calico pony for the hard ride south, his eyes kept cutting to the isolated spot where the pest lodge stood.

Two Twists saw him. "Brother, Tangle Hair and I will need a bit more time to ready our battle rigs. You have heard that Trains the Hawk, my favorite uncle, is among the afflicted. It would mean a great deal to him if our shaman visited the pest lodge and said a brief prayer before he left."

Trains the Hawk was indeed ill. But Tangle Hair was also the unofficial word bringer between Touch the Sky and Honey Eater, as well as Honey Eater's only trusted confidant on the subject of Touch the Sky. He knew full well that Touch the Sky longed to see Honey Eater once more—perhaps for the last time—before he rode out.

Little Horse aided the effort. "Certainly Black Elk will be no problem. He has made it clear that he is indifferent to his wife's fate. Though he hotly declares that she is still his property, and he prates about in her name, huffing out his chest and making brags, he will not visit the lodge."

They were right. Touch the Sky handed his pony's buffalo-hair reins to Two Twists. Then, his throat constricting with nervous anticipation, he crossed to the pest lodge.

Despite his concern for Honey Eater, his feet grew heavy for the last few steps. He could smell the sweet, fragrant incense and hear the children softly crying. Another victim had died, an elder from the silvertip clan. Again, grasping for any straws of hope, Touch the Sky reminded himself that young adults fought the disease longest. And Honey Eater was strong, descended as she was from a long line of great Cheyenne chiefs.

But then he lifted the entrance flap aside. And his hope died when he spotted the woman he loved with all his life. She lay where he had last seen her. But the cruel ravages of mountain fever had already begun to draw the skin of her face tight like green rawhide shrinking in the sun.

Honey Eater was alert, and she recognized him. Her eyes widened in gladness at seeing him. His own heart formed a tight fist of compassionate response when she moved her slim arms over her robe, crossing them at the wrists over her heart—Cheyenne sign talk for love. He quickly crossed his too. But Touch the Sky and Honey Eater both knew this was no place or time for a visit between them alone.

And yet, how much had passed between them! A whole secret life and love patched together in stolen moments and glances, brief exchanges of passionate, and pent-up feelings. Although they had not yet sealed their love's bond by merging their flesh, Honey Eater had finally told him that despite reciting the squaw-taking vows with Black Elk and accepting his bride price, she considered Touch the Sky her only husband. She would violate Cheyenne law and her own great pride and come to him as his wife if he ever sent for her.

But that he would not do, not so long as the

jealous, murderous Black Elk and his spies watched both of them night and day. Touch the Sky scorned any fear for himself. Neither Black Elk nor any other brave would readily close the gap against him. But Honey Eater had already suffered too much because of this love neither one of them could help. And so the two of them suffered on in silence and lived for their secret love, hobbled as it was by cruel reality.

Touch the Sky smiled again at Honey Eater. Then, stepping aside to speak briefly with Sharp Nosed Woman, he reached into his parfleche.

"For Honey Eater," he said. "She cannot pick any fresh ones, and they mean much to her."

He handed Sharp Nosed Woman several clumps of fresh white columbine gently pressed between broad wet leaves.

For a few heartbeats, the weary lines softened in the older woman's face. She nodded and smiled. "I will braid them through her hair myself. Do you know, Touch the Sky, that I once called her a fool for placing little flowers in her hair? If Honey Eater survives this, I will never tease her for it again."

She spoke bravely. But Touch the Sky read the desperation in her tone. Clearly, in her secret heart of hearts, she expected the worst. But hope was a waking dream. As Touch the Sky moved to turn away and say a brief prayer for all, Sharp Nosed Woman laid a hand on his arm.

"Hurry, Touch the Sky," she whispered, "I know

why she loves you, and I approve. I was there when you stood tall and saved the hunt camp from Kiowa and Comanche who meant to steal us for slaves. I watched you swing from the pole without complaint rather than call an addled old grandmother a liar when Wolf Who Hunts Smiling bribed her into a vision against you.

"Some say you once lost our medicine arrows. But if so, did you not scale the cliffs of Wendigo Mountain to get them back? Touch the Sky, if any brave in our tribe can save these dying Cheyennes, it is you. Ride on the wind, tall warrior, and may the high holy ones ride with you. Save them!"

"They have left camp, cousin," Wolf Who Hunts Smiling said, "and they are riding hard. They should reach the Shoshone River before Sister Sun goes to bed."

The young brave had dropped behind to watch their backtrail from a spine of rimrock.

"They had best not plan on passing us," Black Elk said grimly. "That was outright treason during council, bucks. All four of them are enemies of our tribe and our law. Armed enemies."

"Redrock canyons lie ahead," Swift Canoe said. "Perhaps we could hide and kill them there."

Black Elk seemed to consider this plan. But it was Wolf Who Hunts Smiling who spoke up. Some scheme blazed in his wily eyes—one better than Swift Canoe's pale suggestion.

"Never mind such stupid white-skin tricks. How

many times have they failed against this one? And every brave with him is worthy to wear the medicine hat in battle, even young Two Twists. No, never mind the white man's ambush. Better to heap the trouble on them when nature already has them distracted."

Black Elk scowled. "Cousin, you have not one coward's bone in your body. But why do you never speak straight? Take the short way to your meaning. I am a warrior, not a tongue-wagging old squaw."

Wolf Who Hunts Smiling grinned. "As you say, cousin. Well, is this plain enough? I recently scouted this very trail for our hunters. The Shoshone is swollen with runoff and badly flooded. The ford at Crying Horse Bend is fast and dangerous. We must make our move when they are trying to ford the river."

Chapter Five

Touch the Sky's band pushed their mounts hard, bearing south along the ancient trace first blazed by plains hunters and warriors. They knew every water hole in the area and paused only briefly to let their ponies drink at rills and creeks. Luckily their winter-starved horses, after growing weak from nibbling cottonwood bark and old grass trapped under the snow, were in good fettle again from browsing the lush new grass and clover.

The Cheyennes knew that the Shoshone River was often troublesome to ford. Long after the Laramie, the Lodgepole, and other area rivers had receded to their meandering summer levels, the Shoshone still churned white foam well beyond its normal banks. But never had Touch the Sky seen the river so swollen.

"Brothers," Little Horse said as the four braves surveyed the ford at Crying Horse Bend, "can you even tell this was once a wading ford? Last time we crossed here, the water barely trickled over our ponies' fetlocks."

He was forced to shout above the booming roar of the Shoshone. Drift logs, sometimes entire trees, flashed by like a herd of swift animals. The water, muddied by mountain soil, churned and boiled. A huge sawyer had formed in midstream, a vast obstruction of limbs and driftwood and other debris that sawed back and forth in the current.

"Clearly," Tangle Hair said as Touch the Sky dismounted and began searching for sign along the bank, "the river will not be going down any time soon."

"This is the best ford along this stretch of the river," Two Twists said. "There is a better one at Elbow Bend—a sandbar ford that is much easier even in flood weather. But it is a half sleep's ride west of here, well out of our way."

"Unless appearances are dishonest," Touch the Sky said with some wonder in his voice, "then, out of the way or not, Black Elk's band chose Elbow Bend."

Little Horse had been reading the sign too. Now he nodded agreement.

"See here," Touch the Sky said, pointing. "Four ponies rode up to this spot. These many overlapping prints are where they stood. One set of prints goes off to the east. We could follow it to see how far the rider looked for a crossing. But why bother? Here his prints come back again. Nothing was found."

"Nothing," Little Horse said, "and then see where four riders rode west toward Elbow Bend. No prints return. And there is no other place to cross between here and Elbow Bend. So unless they ride back, they will have to cross there."

"They did not cross here," Touch the Sky said. "No prints enter the water."

Little Horse grinned. "Brother, why do you frown? This is an opportunity to be seized. True it is, Cousin River is out for blood. It will be a brisk bit of sport to cross here, no job for children. But I, for one, have no desire to die of old age in my tipi. I am for it. It will give us a good head start."

Despite this bravado, every brave present could not help realizing that drowning was an especially unlucky death for an Indian. A drowning victim's soul remained trapped in the water forever and became a lonely river spirit unable to cross over to the Land of Ghosts.

Touch the Sky glanced around suspiciously at the surrounding terrain: a few low hummocks, a thicket here and there, not much natural cover. But a well-trained Cheyenne who wanted to hide would not need much.

"That is what troubles me," he said. "It will indeed give us a good head start. And who here among us knows either Black Elk or Wolf Who Hunts Smiling to be timid? Black Elk is not as reckless as his cousin, but is it like either of them to avoid this ford?"

Little Horse's grin faded. He caught the drift of his friend's thinking and nodded. "No," he replied. "Neither one of them is such a close friend with caution."

"Not a bit," Tangle Hair said. "Not Black Elk and certainly not Wolf Who Hunts Smiling. But despite his name, Swift Canoe cannot swim, and Stone Mountain's pony is as timid as Stone Mountain is stupid."

Knowing he could not afford to lose a man, Black Elk might well indeed have chosen the safe crossing at Elbow Bend—especially, thought Touch the Sky, if a marksman or two had been left behind to kill their rivals once they entered the river. After all, it was Black Elk who taught young braves in the tribe to shoot game when it was thigh deep in water and could not flee quickly.

A decision had to be made. Touch the Sky's three companions were watching him and waiting. Worse, Honey Eater lay dying while he stood there like a dazed calf, indecisive. But he was reluctant to order this fording. Even the strongest swimmer could drown if he became separated from his mount in that raging current. It was not the Indian way to make important decisions without adequate discussion.

But again Touch the Sky saw Honey Eater

crossing her wrists over her breast. Again he heard the soft whimpers of the sick children. There was no time for long discussions.

"Check your rigs," he said. "Make sure your powder will not get wet, for we may need to burn it soon."

"Cousin River!" Little Horse shouted. "Here come four Cheyennes who never did you harm and always crossed you respectfully. This is for letting us live to see your far bank."

Little Horse had been saving some fine white man's tobacco in his parfleche. He shredded it into the boiling waters as an offering. Tangle Hair tossed in several delicious horehound candies he had traded from a Sioux. Two Twists threw in the last of his coffee beans.

Touch the Sky tossed in his ration of sugar. But he shot a secret glance at Little Horse, wondering if his friend had deliberately not mentioned one more fact that Touch the Sky had gleaned from those prints he'd read: One set of retreating prints was not as deep as the others. Meaning there was no rider on the pony because one brave stayed behind. Touch the Sky had little doubt who that skulking Indian was.

"All right, Cheyennes," he said finally. "Now we ride."

Wolf Who Hunts Smiling waited until the last rider, Tangle Hair, had entered the thundering river. Then, his face divided by the wily smile that was his namesake, he rose up from the shallow pit he had dug behind a spoil bank.

He had been right in his hunch: White Man Runs Him and his band had indeed opted for this dangerous crossing. The brave had convinced Black Elk and the others to cross at Elbow Bend—convinced them, in part, by assuring them he would remain behind to lessen Touch the Sky's numbers and perhaps even kill him. Besides, Stone Mountain's pony refused to enter the water there. And though Stone Mountain did not lack courage to try, he was stupid enough to end up drowning. Black Elk might need him for combat.

Wolf Who Hunts Smiling told the others to lead his mount and leave it hobbled out of sight for him. Now he checked the primer cap in his Colt 1855 rifle. Crouched low, keeping the spoil bank between himself and the river, he held the Colt across his chest and angled toward the raging water.

At first Touch the Sky attempted to keep an eye on the bank behind him as he entered the water. But the current quickly became a powerful foe trying to tear his pony out from under him. It was impossible to fight the river and pay attention to their backtrail.

The four braves formed a wedge, Touch the Sky at the apex. All four spoke to their mounts above the roar, trying to calm and encourage them. But it was all the ponies could do to keep from being sucked under.

In an eyeblink a huge log was bouncing and skipping toward Touch the Sky. The weight and speed of it and the jagged point caused by a break had turned it into a deadly weapon strong enough to pierce the pony's flank.

In a heartbeat Touch the Sky slid hard to one side and jerked hard on one rein, leading the hurtling log by putting his pony at the current's mercy. They floundered, but the maneuver slowed the deadly log's onward thrust just enough for Touch the Sky to hook it with one foot and send it veering. But now he was well downstream from the more narrow spot at the ford. He could glance to the right and spot his three friends—and further behind them Wolf Who Hunts Smiling!

Shock slammed into Touch the Sky even more brutally than the river. The brave on the bank had dropped to one knee and popped the rifle into his shoulder socket, drawing a bead. Somehow, in all the excitement, he must have lost track of the moment when Touch the Sky was swept downstream. Not once did he glance his way—perhaps, thought Touch the Sky, he believed his foe had drowned.

The struggling Cheyenne opened his mouth to shout a warning to his friends. But it was useless against the sustained roar of the Shoshone. He decided to fire a warning shot when, abruptly, the calico was sucked under and Touch the Sky found

Judd Cole

himself staying afloat with one arm while the other desperately tried to hold his Sharps up out of the water. His pony fought her way to the surface, and Touch the Sky managed to remain on her back.

"Brothers!" he screamed. "Behind you!"

But again his voice was lost to the flood-raging river, and now it was too late. The Colt coughed, and Touch the Sky's heart turned over when Tangle Hair's pony suddenly went under in a spray of white foam and blood. A moment later, Two Twists cried out as blood blossomed just above his left elbow. He too plunged into the maelstrom of the river.

The conniving brave on the bank had paused to charge his rifle again. Desperately trying to stay astride his floundering pony, Touch the Sky snapped off a wild shot at his enemy. The bullet kicked up a geyser of dirt near Wolf Who Hunts Smiling, and he flinched violently. He still hadn't spotted his drifting adversary to his left. Concluding a marksman must be hidden somewhere on land, he broke upstream at a run, heading for his hidden pony.

But Touch the Sky grimly realized that the ambitious schemer had inflicted serious damage. Fortunately, Little Horse had been near when Tangle Hair's pony was killed. Little Horse had grabbed for the other brave's arm and gained a purchase. Arms linked over the withers of Little

Horse's pony, they were about to reach the safety of the bank.

The wounded Two Twists, however, was not so fortunate. And even before Touch the Sky could think to act, the youth tumbled past him like a hayseed in the wind. Touch the Sky managed to heave his rifle over to the far bank. But river spray blinded him, and his pony began to wash out from under him. He struck one arm out, felt human flesh, and hung on for dear life. He and Two Twists went under in a tangled confusion of limbs.

Like Touch the Sky's calico, they were on their own. His face taut with the incredible effort, Touch the Sky kicked with his powerful long legs and swam with his free arm. Two Twists made a valiant effort too in spite of his wound.

Just when Touch the Sky feared his strength would give out, hands as strong as an eagle's talons gripped him. Little Horse and Tangle Hair pulled their two friends onto the grassy hump of bank. For some time all four braves lay there, catching their breath. It was Tangle Hair who spoke first. His voice was bitter with rage and loss.

"My best pony dead, already washed out of sight! So is my rifle, my rig."

Touch the Sky took a good look at the Two Twists' wound. "The bullet went through. Soon it will be stiff. But all this cold water slowed the bleeding. If we pack it with balsam and black powder, it will heal well."

Since his friends were safe, rage was settling

into Little Horse's normally placid features. "Did you see him, brothers? Did you? It was Wolf Who Hunts Smiling! He and Black Elk spoke of our treason, yet now they have just shed the blood of their own. Even the thought of the arrows did not hold them back! If he would sully our medicine arrows so boldly, there is no treachery beneath him."

Touch the Sky nodded. His lips were set in a grim, determined slit. "You have caught truth firmly by the tail, buck. There was a time when Black Elk, at least, would not shed tribal blood. But he authorized this attempt at cold-blooded murder."

"As he did, brother," Little Horse said, "when you sojourned at Medicine Lake in quest of your vision."

"Now we know just how it is," Tangle Hair said. "They are murderers, not fellow Cheyennes."

Touch the Sky knew he was right. Black Elk's band were no better than declared enemies to be killed on sight. But despite his anger, Touch the Sky's fear for Honey Eater's life determined his thoughts. Would he ever, he kept wondering with a sharp tug at his stomach, see her alive again?

But their duty lay all before them. And time, like a bird, was on the wing.

"Tangle Hair will take turns riding with all of us," Touch the Sky said. "Check your weapons and prepare to ride."

Chapter Six

Shortly after sunup on the second day after Touch the Sky's band rode out, Seth Carlson spotted a mirror signal from the north.

"It's Trooper Nielson, sir, " Sgt. Reece said. "I posted him out halfway between here and the Shoshone River, at the old freight road station."

"Quiet," Carlson said impatiently. "I'm translating the Morse code." His eyes puckered as he read the quick flashes and the pauses between, spelling out the words. "Four riders coming from river on three horses. Cheyennes. One wounded. Flying truce flag."

Reece laughed a short, hard, derisive bark. "Four riders on three horses! Damn, I'm shittin' my scivvies in fright, sir, my hand to God! And one already wounded for us! This'll be a bird's nest on the ground."

Far less sanguine, Carlson said nothing. He had no proof yet that Matthew Hanchon would be among the approaching Indians. But he knew the Cheyenne's full measure, and in his heart he was convinced Hanchon would make an appeal to Fort Bates. The Indian had yet to discover, however, that his old nemesis Seth Carlson had once again been posted to Fort Bates.

And if Hanchon was coming, Reece was in for some unpleasant lessons about Indian warfare. Carlson hated Hanchon with a passion hotter than hell. But he was also quick to admit the buck had no peer as a fighter.

"Don't dance on his grave too soon," Carlson said.

Once again he glanced carefully about them. The sharpshooters, 40 strong, had taken up positions in two long files, forming a gauntlet between the granite headland of Lookout Bluff and a long, parallel ridge about a hundred yards to the east. The Indian trace passed by below, offering precious little cover as it funnelled into the narrow pass. The terrain hereabouts was too pocked with sand blights and dangerous prairie-dog holes. The Cheyennes would be extremely unlikely to stray wide or ride any other trail.

"I savvy which way you're grazing, sir," Reece said, rubbing a knuckle across his long teamster's mustache. "The Cheyenne—now they're pony-crazy. Almost all their combat training is based on the running skirmish. They run hard and make their opponents chase them until the pursuers' horses founder. Then they turn quick and attack."

Reece grinned. "But the thing of it is, forty marksmen can make the air hum with lead. We're gunna force 'em to hunker down in a fixed position."

Carlson nodded. "Exactly. But that's assuming we don't kill them before they take cover. The men are well within maximum effective range. If they hold and squeeze, the initial surprise volley should do it. I'll bust the first cap as soon as they hit that square clearing where the draw opens out."

As Touch the Sky found himself doing more and more lately, he felt the truth of yet another of Arrow Keeper's favorite sayings: *We must pass through the bitter water before we reach the sweet.* Wolf Who Hunts Smiling's failure to completely stop them at Crying Horse Bend had its good consequences. Surviving that gutsy ford gave the four braves a considerable time advantage over Black Elk's band.

Touch the Sky had made the briefest of pauses to rest the nearly exhausted ponies and their own muscle-strained bodies. By the time Sister Sun had streaked the eastern sky pink, they were again pushing their mounts hard to the south. They were forced to stop more often so that Tangle Hair could leap up behind a new rider. Though Two Twists never once complained, Touch the Sky knew that such a hard pace severely punished his wound.

"There it is, bucks," Little Horse said at that moment, lifting one hand to point ahead in the gathering light of morning. "The ancient headland we call Medicine Mound and the white-skins call Lookout Bluff. Say that name in English, brother."

Touch the Sky did, even as his eyes cut to the white truce flag tied to his lance. Every Cheyenne present knew what he, living among whites as Matthew Hanchon, had learned long ago. By any name, Medicine Mound had long been an observation post for the pony soldiers of Fort Bates. If it was presently manned, he would get a chance to practice his English very soon, assuming a bullet didn't end this mission in a heartbeat.

And it was presently manned. His shaman sense convinced him of that. It hinted at more than that, but he had no luxury to weigh the warning. Was trouble ahead? Trouble was ahead, lurking around the next dogleg bend, ready to pounce. Touch the Sky had no choice. Honey Eater and many more lay dying, while Black Elk and his band were closing in to make more trouble.

Touch the Sky signaled to his comrades, and they dropped back behind him. Again Touch the Sky regretted there was no time to look before they waded in so deep.

Death Camp

As the sun burned off the last mist, the huge granite bluff rose up out of the plains before them. Touch the Sky lifted his lance, peace flag snapping, as the Cheyennes entered the narrow draw between the bluff and the neighboring ridge.

Capt. Seth Carlson's military career had struck some snags these late years, thanks to Matthew Hanchon. But no one in the army denied that Carlson was a seasoned and effective Indian fighter known for molding his troops into crack Indian killers. Units under his command had achieved notable victories against Sioux, Blackfeet, Crow, and Assiniboin. But Hanchon had somehow led a ragtag group of mostly unarmed Cheyennes to a stunning victory over Carlson's mountain regiment in the Bear Paw Mountains.

Carlson's men showed their remarkable discipline as the Cheyennes approached below. Not one broke cover or allowed a piece of brass to glint in the sun. All signals were relayed by hand. And Carlson knew that not one of them would crack a cap until he fired.

The muzzle of his Spencer carbine, well blackened to cut reflection, lay across a low rock in front of him. He had been waiting for the Cheyennes to ride close enough to finally discover if Steele's play with the infected blankets had lured Hanchon.

He raised a pair of field glasses, adjusted the focus, and studied the lead Indian carrying the truce flag. Even from there, with the naked eye, the buck's shoulders looked wide indeed. But with one twist of the focus, Carlson was staring at the face of the man he hated worst of all in the world.

He glanced over at Reece. "Here he comes," he said triumphantly. "It's Hanchon!"

"All due respect, sir, but you're wrong for a fact. It ain't Hanchon. It's two thousand dollars!"

Sharp Nosed Woman was too exhausted, too frustrated, for more tears. She had cried her eyes dry. Her face a frozen mask of resignation, she moved to the entrance of the pest lodge. Her eyes met those of an anxious-looking young mother named Sun Road. Sharp Nosed Woman shook her head. Instantly, Sun Road cried out in overwhelming grief and fell to the ground in a fit of crazy pain.

Just as quickly, following the ancient custom at such times, the women of her clan formed a ring around her for her own protection. No one tried to stop her when she groped in the dirt for a sharp flint and gouged her own arms with it. Even when scarlet ribbons of her blood stained the earth, they did not stop her.

Death was important. Sun Road's infant son had just crossed over, dead from the dreaded fever, and it was right that she marked her terrible loss with pain. The child's life had mattered, and his final agony must be shared. But they would watch her for the next few sleeps, not once letting her lay hands on a more dangerous weapon of self-destruction.

Sharp Nosed Woman turned away and returned to the gloomy interior of the morbid death chamber. The stench of serious illness was powerful, hanging dank in the air like a wet fog. Children cried softly. The older sufferers groaned and begged for water, yet could not hold it down once it was given.

Sharp Nosed Woman stopped and knelt beside Honey Eater. A smaller bundle lay beside her—Honey Eater's little niece Laughing Brook. The child was going rapidly. The pretty little girl's face was drawn as tight as the skin over a knuckle. Like Honey Eater, she had eyes fervid with the destructive fever heat blazing inside them.

"Look," Sharp Nosed Woman said to Honey Eater. "He brought these for you."

She held out the broad leaves with the fresh white columbine petals pressed between them. For a moment, despite the numbing death grip of mountain fever, a surge of joy lessened the suffering in Honey Eater's face.

"Shall I braid them in your hair, charmer? They are always so pretty there."

Honey Eater nodded. When she spoke, her exhausted voice was like a whisper from the spirit world. "But save a few."

She nodded toward little Laughing Brook, who had slipped into unconsciousness. Like her favorite aunt, whom she adored, the little one had several faded columbine petals in her hair.

"The dear little one," Sharp Nosed Woman said, but now a sharp lance of pain broke through her armor of numbness. A sob hitched in her breast and choked off the rest of her words.

Oh, hurry, Touch the Sky, Sharp Nosed Woman prayed silently, watching Honey Eater's wan face. Hurry! Never mind this columbine. Much longer and we will lose the fairest flowers in all the fields.

The morning sun was almost straight overhead when Touch the Sky's band edged into the wide apron of shadow cast by Lookout Bluff. His sense of impending danger was strong. They never should have approached the draw without scouting it first. But urgency made such precautions impossible. The fat was in the fire and it was too late to pull it out. Even so, he stopped his braves for a cautious moment. He had just heard a familiar clicking noise from the edge of the trail.

"I have already heard it, brother," Little Horse said grimly.

All four braves had heard it, and their eyes met in silence. The noises were made by the burrowing of wood-eating insects called deathwatch beetles. Hearing them was a strong omen of impending death.

"Brothers," Little Horse said, craning his neck to stare up above them, "we are not at war with any blue blouses, nor could Black Elk's band have gotten here before us."

He spoke uncertainly, watching Touch the Sky. Little Horse was known for possessing the sharpest senses in the tribe. On a sudden impulse, Touch the Sky said, "Brother, sniff the winds good and tell us what you think."

The rest of them glanced oddly at Touch the Sky. But Little Horse only rode out ahead to a slight rise. He threw back his head, breathed deeply through his nose as he faced the four directions. Then, his face troubled, he rode back to join his friends.

"Earlier I told you I am no reader of thoughts," Touch the Sky said before his friend could speak. "But you smell horses, do you not? Many horses, probably well hidden nearby and muzzled with full grain bags to keep them still."

"Indeed I do, brother," Little Horse replied. "I smell horses rubbed with the stinky liniment used by soldiers."

"They are watching us now, perhaps through bead sights," Touch the Sky said calmly, openly scanning the bluff overhead.

"What about our truce flag?" Tangle Hair said from his spot on the back of Two Twists' pony.

"No one lurks in ambush and hides his horse to show respect to a truce flag," Touch the Sky said. "These tactics mean the attack is coming. They are only waiting for us to clear these shadows and enter that clearing ahead."

"Do we flee back north?" Tangle Hair said.

That seemed the only sane choice. And yet, sane

or not, it also meant sure death for Honey Eater and the rest. For the braves had to pass this point to reach Fort Bates.

Little Horse too realized this fact. "The best way to stop a charging bull is to throw him by the horns. Besides, I would rather be knocked out from under my feather by a bluecoat bullet than swim that angry river again."

Despite their looming threat, Touch the Sky felt a smile tugging at his lips. "Brother," he said fondly, "I believe you are bold enough to count coup on the Wendigo."

"The Wendigo?" Tangle Hair scoffed. "I once borrowed his flint and still have not returned it."

"That is why he killed your pony," Two Twists said, and all four braves tossed back their heads and laughed.

Thus the Cheyennes showed their contempt for the terrible death threat they faced. But it was also the beginning of Touch the Sky's strategy for surviving this trap without retreating.

"All right, bucks," he said. "Break out pemmican and venison. Enjoy your food as we let our ponies set their own pace into the clearing. But watch me and move when I move. Do you see past the clearing to that jumble of scree? We must reach it and cover down until darkness. But from now on, do not look overhead and show no sign that you are anything but hungry. Good luck, brothers, and may the high holy ones ride with us now!"

Chapter Seven

Ever since the tribe learned of the infected blankets, a nubbin of suspicion had been planted in Touch the Sky's mind. As he led his comrades forward toward a hail of lead at any moment, that suspicion was growing into a certainty.

The soldiers hid in ambush above them. Touch the Sky knew full well the entire Cheyenne Nation was at peace with the Great White Father and his Council in Washington. True, isolated bands of the Southern Cheyenne Dog Soldiers were raiding against white-skins. But the Northern Cheyennes had lately suffered only minor run-ins with white settlers and soldiers.

It was a serious violation of the army's standing order, he knew, to attack a peace movement like this. And why would any field commander risk such a serious charge merely to kill four braves riding under a white flag? Even as he asked the question, he knew his old enemy Seth Carlson was back.

"Brothers," he said in a low but clear voice, "a shaman must follow the voices in the wind. Little Horse, are you ready for sport?"

"Is a she-bear with cubs ready for meat?"

"Stout buck! I am going to halt my pony. You continue to ride toward the rocks. Tangle Hair, you and Two Twists follow. Your ponies have all been trained to lie down when commanded. The moment you can do so, get behind the rocks."

Touch the Sky knew his comrades did not approve of his stopping in the sights of many bluecoat guns. But appealing to Little Horse in the name of shamanic power always commanded instant obedience to any order. Little Horse would question no order if Touch the Sky commanded it in the name of higher powers.

"As you say, brother," Little Horse replied in the same low tone. "But I tell you freely, today is not a good day to die. Meet us in the scree."

"I intend nothing else, buck. I have yet to bounce my child upon my knee."

By now all three of his friends had trotted past Touch the Sky. Their hoofclops were echoing down the draw when Touch the Sky shouted overhead in clear English, "Seth Carlson! Before you kill me, I have a message from Kristen Steele!"

Fear of death sent the blood hammering into his

temples. But Touch the Sky sat his calico pony calmly, only squinting a bit to counter the brilliant light of the westering sun. And even through his fear, the anticipation of what he was about to do tempted a grin onto his grim features.

He deliberately waited, watching his friends ease closer to the jumble of scree beside the trail. He was sure he was right about Carlson's being back. Indeed, he could feel the man's surprised indecision, his morbid curiosity, his eagerness to kill his worst enemy in the world held in abeyance by his obsession with the beautiful Kristen Steele. The woman had shamed Carlson forever in his own eyes by preferring an Indian over him.

When Little Horse was almost abreast of the scree, an impatient shout came from above. "Speak your piece quick, Hanchon. The buzzards are gettin' hungry!"

Touch the Sky knew the order to fire was about to come. It was now or never. He must time his words just right.

"Yes, sir, Capt. Bluecoat, sir," he replied, his tone openly mocking. "She told me to tell you that any decent white woman would chose to mate with a Cheyenne dog before she'd kiss your filthy lips! Jump, bucks!" he added in Cheyenne.

Carlson had been expecting nothing like this. He was so hot and weak with unbelieving rage that he couldn't see through the red haze of his anger. That rage swelled his throat shut, and no order came out immediately, only an empty swallow. The momentary delay was costly to the soldiers. Below, the three Cheyennes in the lead suddenly slid to the ground and whacked their ponies on the rump, sending them into the scree.

At the same moment, Touch the Sky dug sharply at his pony's flanks, surging forward. Simultaneously, he slid forward and down, into the famous Cheyenne defensive riding posture. He clung low on the pony's neck, swinging much of his body behind the horse.

"Fire!" Carlson finally managed, his own Spencer kicking into his shoulder as he wildly jerked the trigger, anger making him waste the round.

The calico was trained to flee in zigzagging patterns at the sound of gunfire. Carlson had failed to direct his men's fire toward Hanchon. Since Hanchon was clearly dead meat, most of them instead took desperate shots at the braves who were disappearing into the rocks.

Touch the Sky clung on for dear life as his pony surged toward cover. Bullets thwacked into the ground all around him, but not as many as he'd feared. He could hear Carlson cursing at his men, redirecting their fire.

Then, his jaw dropping in astonishment, Touch the Sky saw Two Twists leap back out from the cover of the scree. With a shout of utter disdain, the young brave stood in the open and lifted his clout at the bluecoats—an Indian gesture of pure contempt which always infuriated hair-face soldiers. Ignoring their C.O., many took aim at the gutsy youth.

Then Touch the Sky reached the jumble of scree. Little Horse leapt out, grabbed Two Twists, and tugged him back to cover. Touch the Sky bounced to the ground, came up on his feet, and whacked his pony on the rump. Then the same momentum that let him succeed in his strategy finally threw him to a hard landing among the scree.

"Welcome, Cheyenne!" Little Horse greeted him. Pride clear in his tone, he added, "Did you see young Two Twists here? I will personally add another feather to his bonnet. That was the finest coup I have seen in many moons. Either he is courageous or soft brained!"

"Crazy or brave," Touch the Sky shouted above the whang of ricocheting bullets, "either one will do for a warrior!"

Despite the warriors' bravado, however, Touch the Sky knew they were truly up against it this time. Hours of daylight remained. The soldiers held the valuable high ground. The Cheyennes were pinned down, trapped, forced to fight the way they hated to.

They were well enough protected for the moment, but only if they hugged the scree tight and stayed out of sight. The least glimpse at one of them from above sent bullets hurtling into their position.

Seth Carlson! Touch the Sky tasted bitter bile at the thought of locking horns with his old enemy when time was of the essence and Honey Eater and many more lay dying. Black Elk and Wolf Who Hunts Smiling were obstacles enough for any man. Now his most deadly paleface enemy was tossed into the potlatch.

Now and then, without warning or pattern, the soldiers would unleash another volley from overhead. In a lull between volleys, Touch the Sky saw Little Horse frown. All of them lay hugging the ground. That was why Touch the Sky soon felt it too—the faint vibration of riders passing.

"Brothers!" Little Horse said, barely lifting his head to peer toward the east. "Black Elk and his band have been warned by the bluecoat rifles. There they go, bearing toward Fort Bates!"

This only increased Touch the Sky's desperation. For if allowed to carry out his reckless plan to take hostages, Black Elk would ruin any chance for a mercy appeal to the fort. The sick ones back at camp were surely doomed then.

"What do we do?" Tangle Hair said. "It is a standoff now. We cannot move, nor can the soldiers come down off the bluff without giving us clear shots at them on an uncovered slope. They could rush us, but many would die."

"They will not rush us," Touch the Sky said. "Such a foolish move would leave many widows and orphans back east of the Great Waters. No, they plan to wait. They have food enough for many sleeps. We have only what is in our sashes and parfleches."

Little Horse nodded. "As you say, they plan to wait. What do we plan to do, shaman?"

"The only thing left for us to do," Touch the Sky said glumly. "We wait until Sister Sun has gone to rest. The white skins will send men down. Let them. We are going to slip past them in the darkness."

As soon as the last glow of day bled from the western horizon, both the soldiers and the Cheyennes went into action. Fortunately for the Indians, it was a cloudy night with no moon or stars visible. Despite the soldiers' caution, Touch the Sky could hear their equipment noises as they deployed on foot down off the bluff. Moving quickly, the four Cheyennes dropped farther back into the scree and recruited their ponies. They muzzled them with their sashes, wrapped their hoofs in rawhide. The braves had darkened their own bodies by rubbing dirt into saliva to make a mud paste.

Prior to sunset, they had wrapped their eyes tight and remained in total darkness for a long time. This forced them to be especially vigilant with their ears to detect movement from above. But it also gave them excellent night vision once they unwrapped their eyes. Now they could make out shapes at distances they never could have managed normally.

Thus giving themselves a tiny advantage, they led their ponies step by agonizing step through the rocks. Now and then Touch the Sky made out the vague shape of a soldier who could not see him. It was a harrowing exodus, every breath capable of warning their enemy.

But Maiyun smiled on his red children that night. After what seemed a tense eternity, they had outflanked the baffled soldiers and even discovered their hidden rope corral. They stole a sturdy roan for Tangle Hair and resumed their desperate ride toward Fort Bates.

There could be little elation at thus eluding the soldiers because Black Elk's lead was daunting. Touch the Sky was desperate for any plan that might cut that lead. The possible solution presented itself when they broke over the crest of a ridge and spotted a well-lit camp below.

It was more bluecoats, a large work detail of log cutters. Several huge squad fires were burning, flames sawing in the wind and illuminating small groups of soldiers everywhere. A railroad spur track ended at the camp. Several flatbed cars were piled high with fresh-cut pine logs.

But something else caught and held Touch the Sky's eye: two mobile wagons, loaded with wires and equipment, which the army called a Flying Telegraph Train. These contained the equipment, including an electromagnetic generator, for the portable telegraph system known as the Beardslee Telegraph. Touch the Sky had learned of them during his last days among the whites when the machines were first introduced. The mobile unit could splice into any telegraph wire, and several passed through this area. But his companions knew none of this.

"Here is more trouble," Little Horse said. "We must circle wide around them. More time out of our way."

"Not at all," Touch the Sky said promptly. "These blue blouses are timely met. You three are going to rest here a moment with the ponies. I am riding down to counsel with their soldier chief."

"Brother," Tangle Hair said, "lately you make great sport of presenting yourself as a target for bluecoats."

"Truly," Little Horse said. "I thought you were keen to catch Black Elk's group before they ruin our mission?"

"Just so." Touch the Sky nodded down toward the Flying Telegraph, clearly outlined in the ample orange-yellow glow from camp. "Those are not freight wagons. The soldiers can use them to send words through the talking wire."

"This talking wire," Two Twists said dubiously. "I have heard the lines humming like spring bees. But surely such powerful magic is not real?"

"As real as that bullet Wolf Who Hunts Smiling sent through your arm, buck. With luck, the talking wire will stop Black Elk long before we could. Wait here, brothers, and only hope these soldiers follow a better leader than Seth Carlson."

Touch the Sky let his pony walk closer. The soldiers were too numerous—and too well armed—to fear attacks, so no sentries had been posted. When the brave was perhaps a double stone's throw away from the camp circle, he called out from the trees, "Hello, the camp! Friend approaching with a message. Permission to enter your camp?"

The talking and singing ceased; a banjo fell silent. A lieutenant stepped out of a wedge tent, his blouse unbuttoned.

"Civilian or soldier?" the officer called out.

After the slightest hesitation, Touch the Sky replied, "Soldier, sir."

"Advance and be recognized, trooper!"

Touch the Sky swallowed the nervous lump in his throat. He nudged the calico with his knees, speaking quietly in her ear to calm her at all these new sights and smells. They moved into the dim edge of the firelit circle, then farther and farther into the light.

Exclamations followed them like dominoes falling.

"Holy Saint Francis!"

"Well, I'll be go to hell!"

"Injuns!"

"Mebbe it's a trick and we're being attacked!"

"Hold your damn horses," Touch the Sky said. "You boys got the eyeballs God gave you? This is a truce flag, not a wiping patch. How many wild savages do you know who palaver English like I'm doing right now? I've got three comrades sitting back there behind me, tired and hungry. Even if you don't give a hoot in hell for our red asses, I'm asking for mercy in the name of our women and children."

"You men!" the lieutenant barked. "Stack those rifles before you shoot somebody, you damned fools! I don't know what this red son is up to. Even if he's trying to bamboozle some grub out of us, he's no hostile. A fool, maybe, but no hostile. Who's your message from?"

"It's not from anybody. It's going to Fort Bates. You need to send a telegram, sir. Right now a band of marauding Cheyennes are heading that way along the old Sioux Trace. They plan to take hostages from among the settlers, then force Fort Bates to cooperate."

"If that's straight goods, then they're fools. Col. Neusbaum is one hard case. He barely negotiates a point with Washington, let alone hostile Indians." The officer looked at Touch the Sky askance. "You're a Cheyenne too, aren't you?"

When Touch the Sky nodded, he said, "I've seen the Apaches sell out their own for tobacco and such. I thought Cheyennes were tighter than that."

"We are. It is not easy for even the most errant Cheyenne to lose his place with us, so reluctant are we to forsake our own. Even some murderers may live among us, though in shame forever. But one crime we will not forgive is treason against the People. Some of the men in this group are traitors who have killed their own merely to acquire power."

Quickly, Touch the Sky explained the emergency back at the Powder River camp. At the mention of mountain fever, the front ring of troopers crowded back away from this new arrival.

"Don't worry," Touch the Sky said. "I'll stay back. But if these Cheyenne traitors strike first, I lose all chance for any help from the fort. You could not only warn the fort about this attack. You could also tell them that I helped you and that I'm on the way for help myself."

The young officer looked unsure. "The thing of it is, I got no kick if you're telling the straight. But I ain't putting paid to any deal before I got a little more information. How come your English is so good? You didn't learn that English at a reservation school."

"No, my name was once Matthew Hanchon. I grew up in Big Horn Falls."

"Hanchon? John Hanchon's adopted boy?"

When Touch the Sky nodded, somebody spoke up from the circle of gawking soldiers. "By Godfrey! It is Matthew Hanchon!"

A sergeant with ample folds of belly drooping over his blue kersey trousers stepped into the light. "Good God, you've put on some growth, tadpole! Collected you some fine battle scars too, I see. You recollect my ugly face? Use to was, I'd buy you a licorice stick from the sutler every time you brought a load out to the fort from your folks' store."

"Tosh Blackford!" Touch the Sky said promptly. "You used to make plenty of money getting the troopers to bet on fights between red and black ants."

"Hell, he still robs us that way, the damn piker!" a trooper groused.

"Shut your gob, Peyton," Blackford said affably. He turned to the officer. "Lt. Westphal, I'll vouch for this lad, Injun or no. He's straight grain, clear through."

"Good enough for me, Sergeant. I was convinced when I found out he's John Hanchon's boy. If there's a better man in Bighorn Falls, I've yet to meet him. Trooper Crawford!"

"Sir!"

"Put that scouse down. You can feed your face later. Right now, go fire that Beardslee up."

"Yes, sir!"

Lt. Westphal looked at Touch the Sky. "I know Indians don't like saying their names in front of palefaces, so I'll just call you Matthew. Quick, now, tell me more about the Indians ahead of you."

Chapter Eight

"There it is, Panther Clan," Wolf Who Hunts Smiling said to Black Elk. "One of those paleface lodges below is where Woman Face grew up wearing shoes."

"I have been here," Swift Canoe boasted. "I spied on White Man Runs Him when he played the fox alongside his white-skin soldier brothers. If River of Winds had not stopped me, I would have sent him across."

"Many would have done so," Black Elk scoffed. "You two have failed. Remember this. I alone have not yet closed for the kill against him. We two have locked horns, yes, but always the thought of the arrows held us back. Now it no longer matters. For he has the arrows, and thus they are no longer clean. And when I do close to kill him, there will

92

be no would about it. It will be done and soon."

"I already know you as a war leader, cousin," Wolf Who Hunts Smiling said. "Now I know you as a speaker too. I have placed your words in my sash for they have weight and importance."

While he said this, the younger brave held his face impassive and gazed with the others down from the rimrock at the moonlit river valley. But inside he smiled in elation at Black Elk's deeply bitter tone. The insidious worm of jealousy had burrowed deep into Black Elk's heart, poisoning it, turning him from a hard but fair warrior into one obsessed by a murderous rage against Touch the Sky—and perhaps Honey Eater too. Wolf Who Hunts Smiling had worked tirelessly, often secretly, to nurture that evil, gnawing worm inside Black Elk.

Black Elk had to be ruined, for he was loyal to Chief Gray Thunder and too strong to be ignored. In his own way, he was nearly as dangerous to Wolf Who Hunts Smiling's ambition as was Touch the Sky himself. Both would die a hard death. With the Comanche Big Tree and the Blackfoot Sis-ki-dee joining their renegade bands with him, no fort would stop them. Then the lush green grass of the plains would be awash in paleface blood when the war to exterminate them began.

Black Elk had lost some of his lusty vigor as a leader; he had become an intense brooder as his hatred deepened. Like the cowardly women he often berated, he had lately begun to express his hatred more in words against his enemy.

"Had we time enough," he said, "I would learn which lodge was his and steal the white fools who raised him. After they had served as hostages, I would kill them anyway. We owe it to them. In keeping Woman Face alive, they dealt death to our tribe.

"However, with luck Woman Face is worm fodder by now. Those blue blouses had him pinned like a snake under a wheel. As for us, we must settle for the first white skins who are for the taking."

"Indeed," Swift Canoe said, "any will do. Once the long knives know Indians have seized even one of their dogs, they will go to Wendigo in their wrath."

"You speak straight arrow," Stone Mountain said. His flat buffalo-hide saddle creaked when the huge Indian shifted to look at the others. "Whites do not suffer such treatment lightly."

Black Elk's face twisted in rage and contempt. He stared at both the speakers. "What? Would these two quivering maidens rather be gathering onions and nuts with the women? This is a warrior's mission, bucks."

"I have never picked onions," Swift Canoe said resentfully.

"Nor I," Stone Mountain said. "True it is, I once helped the women stretch meat onto the drying racks, but—"

"You tangle-brained fools!" Wolf Who Hunts

Death Camp

Smiling said. "A rabbit could not find a full brain between you."

"Leave it alone, cousin," Black Elk said with disgust. "You are right, but why lecture rabbits?"

But something had caught Black Elk's sharp eyes even as he spoke. His wary attention alerted the others. He pointed to a narrow defile in a ridge to the east. A squad of soldiers debouched, racing toward the Cheyenne position. The cloud cover had blown off recently, and they were clear enough in the silver-white moonwash.

"And look there!" Swift Canoe added, pointing to the cluster of frame buildings comprising Bighorn Falls. Suddenly the main street swarmed with shadows—no doubt more mounted soldiers.

"They have somehow been warned of our arrival!" Black Elk said. "We have lost the advantage of surprise. And now we must lose more time shaking these gnats."

Already the first carbines were spitting orange licks of flame. Black Elk yanked his pony around.

"Now we must rely on the second plan we discussed. We will split up and lose them out on the plains. Do not waste ammunition firing upon them. Just outride them. Then we will recruit at the white-skin wagon road. Soon it will be light and traffic will be heavy there. Warning or no, we will seize hostages and force the blue blouses to give us their powerful medicine."

* * *

"I'm damned if I know how they got away, sir," Sgt. Nolan Reece apologized. "But they're gone for a fact. We've turned over every rock in that scree. Hanchon and the rest of them red Arabs slipped off slicker'n grease through a goose."

"You still so all fire sure it's a bird's nest on the ground?" Carlson demanded. "Damn it all, soldier, we've been here hours with our thumbs up our sitters, and who knows how long they've been riding."

"Well, you said he was a slippery bastard," Reece said lamely. " 'Pears to me you was right. Him and every buck with him."

"Sir!" a corporal called out, snapping off a salute as he rushed up to Carlson. "The men are standing by their mounts as you ordered. But McQuady's horse is gone. Them Cheyennes must've boosted it!"

Carlson cursed again. He turned back to Reece.

"We can't let Hanchon get to the fort. Col. Neusbaum is no Indian lover. But he's a rule-book commander. And the rule-book says a request for humanitarian aid should be honored if possible, even when it's from savages. Once Neusbaum knows about the epidemic, we can't touch Hanchon or his bunch."

"So what's the plan, sir?"

"Sweat and guts, man! Their horses are tired. Ours are fresh and strong from grain and good graze. We'll push our mounts hard and try to catch them. If we can, I swear they won't shake us again."

Despite the unexpected friendly reception at the bluecoat work camp, Touch the Sky knew they still had a long, dangerous ride to Fort Bates. Desperation had settled deep into his features. Already nearly two sleeps had passed. Delays had cut the already dangerous margin even shorter. Honey Eater might already be dead and the rest past all help. Lt. Westphal's telegram would indeed help. At least the fort knew why the braves were coming. With incredible luck, with unquestioning cooperation from the soldiers, there might still be time.

But one more serious delay, and the Powder River camp could be beyond all help. With Honey Eater's death, he would lose his main reason for all this suffering and fighting to survive.

That meant he could make no careless assumptions—especially the assumption that the warning telegram guaranteed Black Elk's band would be removed as a threat. And Carlson was out there somewhere too, meaner than the white man's Satan with a sunburn.

So as they followed the old Sioux Trace south toward the fort, he relied on a scouting trick once the morning sun was up. Despite the additional loss of time, he halted his band several times to hastily climb a tall tree. From there, he kept a wary eye on both their backtrail and the road ahead. Thus it was that he spotted double danger approaching them like the tongs of a deadly pincers closing.

"Brothers," he called down, "trouble on the hoof, and enough for all!"

Ahead, toward the fort, he could see a clear stretch of the freight road. A stagecoach rocked and bounced, making its way south toward Bighorn Falls. The passengers' carpetbags and portmanteaus bulged out from under the leather boot. The four-horse team strained against their tug chains, fighting a long slope. And hidden in a cutbank at the top of the slope was Black Elk's band!

As if that weren't enough trouble, more bad news approached from behind them. Seth Carlson's platoon raced along a second trail in sets of four, their swallow-tail unit guidon snapping in the breeze.

Touch the Sky needed no shamanic eye to see that Black Elk intended to seize the passengers as hostages. He glanced again at his Cheyenne enemies. Then he shifted on the tree limb to once more study his white enemy.

They couldn't have spotted each other yet. Touch the Sky estimated how fast the soldiers were approaching. Then he guessed how much time remained before the stagecoach reached that cutbank. And all at once, despite seeming hopelessness, a grin split his face.

"Little Horse," he called down, "are you as crazy as you boast?"

"None crazier. Test my fettle, buck!"

"Then I shall. We are about to offer ourselves as free targets to the bluecoats!"

Rapidly, Touch the Sky climbed down. He explained the situation to his comrades. "Brothers," he concluded, "there is no time to keep fighting these running battles. "Let us see if we can lure one enemy onto another."

The trail Carlson's unit currently rode would take them wide of Black Elk and the stagecoach. Touch the Sky's band quickly mounted and rode straight into the teeth of Carlson's advance.

When he was sure they'd been spotted, Touch the Sky doubled back toward the freight road, which wound to the southwest of Carlson's current position. He looked back over his shoulder and watched both columns veer in his direction.

"They have taken the bait!" Little Horse gloated. "Now we will give them a merry chase, brothers!"

Despite these bold words, however, Touch the Sky knew the chase would be anything but merry. Their Indian ponies were the pluckiest on the plains. But they had been ridden hard lately and had rested little, they were nearly exhausted from covering too much ground in too little time. The big cavalry horses, in contrast, were strong and sleek, well grazed and rested.

Several more razorback ridges had to be crossed before the soldiers would be able to spot the stagecoach and the drama unfolding on the freight road. In the meantime, Carlson's veteran

Indian Killers were closing the gap. At first the pursuers' rifle shots had sounded like the insignificant popping of chokecherries. The rifle cracks grew louder, and the fleeing Cheyennes heard bullets fly past their ears with angry-hornet sounds.

"Hi-ya!" Little Horse shouted, thoroughly enjoying this sport. "All they can do is kill us, brothers! Fall on enemy bones!" He raised his streamered lance and shook it at the hair-face soldiers. "Hiii-ya!"

Touch the Sky felt the game little calico's muscles straining beneath him. Now and then wet foam blew back onto him as she started to lather from the pace.

The next time he glanced back, he spotted Seth Carlson's determined face under the turned-up brim of his officer's hat. The soldier's eyes stabbed back, sheening with livid hatred. He was focused on the Cheyenne buck like a bobcat on its prey.

A bullet whanged past Touch the Sky's ear, chipping bark off a nearby cottonwood. The calico was blowing harder, starting to slow noticeably. Once she nearly stumbled.

The cavalry thundered so close that Touch the Sky could see divots of ground being ripped loose by their horses' iron-shod hoofs. Now, Touch the Sky knew, came the most delicate part of this maneuver. It would be a tricky combination of feinting and timing.

When the braves topped the last ridge, Touch the Sky spotted the stagecoach again. It was perhaps a double stone's throw from the cutbank where Black Elk's band were hidden, waiting to pounce. Touch the Sky hoped to expose the attack after it was under way, but before the driver or shotgun were killed.

He watched the stage roll closer and heard the thunder gathering behind his band as the troopers pressed on. The air was deadly with bullets, and the Cheyennes were riding in their low-and-forward defensive postures.

However, Touch the Sky's timing was perfect. Black Elk's band shot forth from the cutbank, yipping, even as Carlson crested the ridge and spotted this new trouble.

For a moment Touch the Sky again met his white enemy's eyes. He read the agony of indecision there. Clearly Carlson longed, with all his heart, to continue dogging his enemy until he had finally killed him. But just as clearly, even an officer as corrupt as he could not forsake such an obvious duty. How would he explain, if anyone on the stagecoach survived, why he had let renegades attack innocent civilians?

Even from there, Touch the Sky could read the curse on Seth Carlson's lips. Mocking him with his eyes, Touch the Sky led his band off toward the southwest.

Carlson and his troops continued on toward the freight road. The bugler blasted out *Boots and Saddles* to hearten the victims and frighten the attackers. While one enemy thus routed the other,

Touch the Sky and his loyal comrades raced toward Fort Bates.

But despite this elating victory over two enemies, Touch the Sky did not feel like reciting coups. After all, telegram or no, they were still approaching the soldier house of enemies. Nor could he stop seeing the image of Honey Eater's feverdrawn face and wondering over and over if he would ever see her alive again.

Chapter Nine

No one at Fort Bates had yet learned about the aborted Indian attack on the stagecoach bound for Laramie. Seth Carlson's platoon was officially listed in the company roster as on extended maneuvers. He was not expected back at Fort Bates until rations ran low. Unwilling to forego one more chance at killing Hanchon, Carlson did not want to report his action and risk being detained in garrison. He ordered his men into a bivouac near Beaver Creek.

Meantime, Fort Bates remained in a state of high alert. A telegram from Lt. Westphal had warned of an attack on the settlement of Bighorn Falls by desperate Cheyenne renegades. Two rifle companies had been dispatched to patrol the valley. So far, neither had returned.

The morning was still young when Pvt. Colin Padgett and Pvt. Hoby Cunninghan reported for four hours of guard duty at the main gate of Fort Bates. This was one of the last walled forts on the frontier, an enclosure of spiked cottonwood logs with gun towers at each corner.

The huge, iron-reinforced front gate was always kept open since serious threats from Indians had been eliminated in this sector. Padgett and Cunningham stood just outside the open gate, their carbines at sling arms.

"Lord, this dust does get thick on a man's tongue," Padgett said, winking at his comrade. He uncapped his bull's-eye canteen and took a hasty swig from it.

Even from six feet away, Cunningham could smell the strong odor of cheap 40-rod.

"Ahh, rock me to sleep, mother," Padgett said, smacking his lips in appreciation. He glanced back over his shoulder toward the company office, then passed the canteen to Cunningham.

Duty on the frontier was deadly boring—long hours and days and weeks of monotony punctuated by sudden violence. Things were so bad that one-third of all new recruits took French leave, as deserting was called. Those who stuck it out often fell victim to Old Knockumstiff, which the wily Fort Sutler always had ready to hand.

The corporal of the guard had informed both sentries of the special orders concerning a renegade band of Cheyenne loose in the territory.

Death Camp

Somehow, though, the news about a second Cheyenne band approaching the fort for assistance had never reached the guards. So Padgett's voice tightened an octave with nervousness when he suddenly said, "Damn my eyes! Look out there!"

He pushed himself away from the wall he'd been resting against and unslung his carbine. He pointed out across the vast and rolling scrubland.

Cunningham squinted. "I can't tell a Cheyenne from the Queen of England. But them's Injuns, and four of 'em, just like we was warned."

"They're Cheyennes," Padgett said when the band had moved even closer, dust puffs rising behind their horses. "Those are black feathers in their bonnets. Crow feathers. Sioux wear white feathers."

A moment later, squinting against the distance, Padgett added a long whistle. "Damn, boys! One of 'em's riding a cavalry hoss! They've killed at least one trooper!"

Padgett had gone on some scouting details, but neither private had yet faced combat. The army of that day figured it was cheaper to replace a man than to train him. Consequently, neither trooper had ever actually fired the new seven-shot Spencer carbines they'd been issued.

"The crazy red bastards just keep a'comin!" Cunningham explained. "They can't be soft brained enough to attack a fort, can they?"

"The hell they can't! It's a suicide mission!"

Padgett said. "That white rag don't mean jack. Shut the gate!"

The tower guards had spotted the riders racing toward the post too. Cunningham and Padgett quickly unlooped the ropes holding the gate open and swung it closed, dropping the huge wooden bar. The gate was loopholed to allow for defensive fire.

"We're being attacked!" Padgett shouted toward a knot of soldiers just then emerging from the messhall. "On the line, we're being attacked!"

The soldiers scrambled, racing toward the armory, where the enlisted men kept their weapons when not in the field or on guard duty. A moment later, the first shots rang out from the gun towers.

As his band approached Fort Bates, Touch the Sky had not been unduly alarmed. Even from far back, he could see that the gate stood open as usual, and no soldiers were patrolling outside.

Indeed, it was difficult to focus his attention on the fort. Returning to the river valley where he had been raised had planted a sharp spike of nostalgia inside his breast. If only things were different, he could have visited his white parents on their mustang spread. And though Kristen Steele was long gone, this was where he had met and fallen in love with her. Lost is such reflections, and mired in worry for Honey Eater, he didn't realize the new danger until Tangle Hair's shout roused him.

"Brothers! They are closing the soldier town against us!"

Only then did the tall brave see the gate swinging shut. He should have halted his band, he thought. But halt them to do what? Waste more time they couldn't afford to waste? A white flag flew from his lance, clear for all to see. Lt. Westphal had telegraphed ahead. There was nothing else for it. They must gain the fort and get help or die trying.

Touch the Sky didn't see the first muzzle puffs as the tower guards commenced firing. But he was fully aware when a bullet ripped through the truce flag, leaving a hole dead center. Plumes of dirt shot up all around them as the tower sentries opened up in earnest.

The Cheyenne ponies began their defensive zigzagging, making it difficult for the enemy to lead their targets when aiming. But Touch the Sky realized it was already too late to turn back. Yet each step hurled them closer to death and the end of all hope for Honey Eater and the tribe.

Capt. Tom Riley was one of the first soldiers to hear the shouts and shooting from the south wall. He had just finished the morning formation of his company. Now he was seated in the officers' mess over a plate of sourdough biscuits and side meat when the racket broke out.

Riley had only recently been posted back to Fort Bates after a long stint of duty down south on the

Llano Estacado, or Staked Plain, Comanche country. He had served here early in his career as a mustang lieutenant promoted by brevet from the enlisted ranks. In recognition of superior service and courage in battle, his brevet rank had become permanent.

As he raced toward the gate, unsnapping the holster of his cavalry .44, suspicion bothered him. Riley knew what Lt. Westphal's telegram had said about the renegade Cheyenne Indians. But never did he suspect which Cheyenne was among those approaching the fort until he peeked out the Judas hole in the gate.

"You idiots!" he snapped at Padgett and Cunningham. "I know you two are fresh fish when it comes to combat. But don't you know the rules of engagement? Never fire on a truce flag!"

"Sir, we got orders."

"Trooper, you're out of line! You have new orders now. Open that damn gate or I'll have you doing barrel drill all night!"

His face red with anger, Riley turned toward the two south-facing towers. "Cease fire! Cease fire, you hayseed halfwits! Those are friendlies!"

Padgett didn't look too happy, but he threw the gate open again and then backed off with his weapon raised.

"Lower that piece, trooper!" Riley snapped. "Don't point a weapon at a man unless you mean for sure to kill him. Besides, I can see from here you haven't got a round in the chamber. Did you

Death Camp

trade your ammo for rotgut whiskey again from that thieving sutler?"

Padgett noticed his empty chamber and blushed pink clear to his earlobes. "Hell, I had me a bullet in there, sir," he muttered sheepishly.

But Riley waved him off with a disgusted shake of his head. He turned around and ordered the men now assuming battle positions to stand down and secure their weapons.

The Indians pressed onward, if anything deliberately increasing their speed in defiance as they neared the fort. Dust boiled up behind their ponies, and the nearly exhausted animals blew foam. Then they flew through the wide gate at a dead run, scattering slow and surprised soldiers like driftwood in a flood. Then the ponies stopped as if on cue, in half the distance a cavalry horse would have needed.

Touch the Sky's face showed nothing as he surveyed the ring of gawping soldiers. Then his eyes met Riley's, and in spite of his warrior training, a glad smile divided his face.

"Tom Riley!"

"Mrs. Riley's best-looking boy at your service."

Riley deliberately avoided saying Touch the Sky's Cheyenne name, knowing Indians believed their names lost their medicine when heard by white ears. "I heard about Westphal's telegram. So your tribe's up against it?"

Touch the Sky nodded grimly. "You've heard enough, I see. Good, because there's no more time for talk. It may already be too late."

Riley nodded. "C'mon. I'll take you to Col. Neusbaum right now. I'll warn you. He's a better man than some the Army is sending out here to command forts. But he sure's hell ain't no friend of the red man."

When Tom Riley finished hastily explaining the situation, Col. William Neusbaum nodded with a distracted air. He looked across his wide, immaculate desk at the dirty and wild-looking Indian standing in front of him. Old blood stained the fringes of Touch the Sky's leggings, and a violent history was told in the many knife and burn scars covering his chest and back. So far the Cheyenne had said nothing, respectfully holding back despite a desperate urgency clear in his eyes.

"You say he speaks some English?" Neusbaum said doubtfully to Riley.

"Yes, sir." Riley added tactfully, "I'm sure you could talk right to him, sir, instead of through me. It would save time."

Neusbaum grunted at this response. He was in his early fifties, a heavy-jowled man with thick silver hair plastered back by pomade. He spoke with exaggerated enunciation, slowly and raising his voice as if to an imbecile. "Pleased to meet you." After a moment's hesitation, he offered his hand across the desk.

"Uhh, sir," Riley said, "Indians don't shake—"

"Oh, hell," Touch the Sky said, taking the colonel's hand in a powerful grip, "there's no time for all that, Tom! Colonel, it's a very sincere pleasure to make your acquaintance. My chief, Gray Thunder, sends his respect. He thanks you straight from his heart for doing a far better job than the other eagle chiefs sent here before you. He told me you are the first to enforce the treaty that keeps white miners off our land without our permission."

At this clearly spoken English, Col. Neusbaum stared as if a dog had just sung "The Homespun Dress." The surprise turned to a brief smile at the compliment. "Well, you tell Gray Thunder we've had no trouble from his band. I appreciate that. This business with your people, it's very unfortunate. But there's a problem. The U.S. Army does not have its own medical corps or doctors out here. We contract with civilian surgeons. I can't order a contract surgeon to do anything that's not in his contract. And the contracts say nothing about helping savage—uh—I mean, Indians."

"Sir," Riley said, his tone more urgent, "are you sure we couldn't put a little more priority on this. Maybe we could arrange something with Dr. Ladislaw?"

Neusbaum's eyebrows shot up in annoyed surprise at Riley's peremptory tone. Riley was not one to gainsay his superiors. But Neusbaum decided to let his irritation pass. Riley was the best officer on his staff, and good officers should be humored now and then. And this Cheyenne smelled bad, but he was likable enough.

"At ease, Captain. I've sent for Ladislaw. We'll see what he says."

Even as he finished speaking, several quick knocks made all three heads turn toward the open office door. A civilian wearing a faded leather weskit stepped into the room. Dr. Hinton Ladislaw was about ten years younger than Neusbaum, a balding man with timid eyes and a string-bean build. He shrank back, startled, at sight of the tall Cheyenne. Clearly he was a greenhorn around Indians and wished to remain that way.

Quickly, Col. Neusbaum explained the situation. "How 'bout it, Hinton?" Neusbaum said when he'd finished. "You willing to take some medicine and go back to their camp with it?"

Ladislaw's jaw suddenly dropped. "Go to an Indian camp?"

When the Colonel nodded, Ladislaw shook his head like a man who didn't like the look of a horse's teeth. " 'Fraid not, Bill. I didn't take this job so I could get separated from my topknot or what's left of it, anyhow. I don't know much about Indians, but I've heard they kill a medicine man if he fails. You say it's been several days now since the fever hit. There's a damn good chance it's already too late. I'm not too eager to put my bacon in the fire for a lost cause."

Riley was about to object. But Touch the Sky,

his face and voice fighting back the frustration, beat him to it.

"Dr. Ladislaw, listen to me. I promise on my life that no one will hurt you, no matter what happens. I and my friends waiting outside will see to that. Sir, you're a doctor. You took an oath, and nothing in that oath said that Indians don't count. I know that my people and your people have often raised our battle-axes against each other. But we Cheyennes never take the fight to your women and children or let any whites die of disease if we can help.

"This last winter was hard. My tribe was short of meat and firewood. But when a white-skin wagon train foolishly set out from the settlements too late, getting caught in the mountains all winter, we kept the people alive until the spring melt. We were not happy about it; many of us grumbled. But we did it."

Ladislaw had heard about this from the survivors. The heartfelt appeal clearly touched him.

"Aw, won'tcha, Hinton?" Riley said. "I'll give you that little sorrel mare you're so sweet over."

Hinton looked at Neusbaum. The colonel was getting caught up in the appeal too as he listened to this young Indian who mingled manly respect with a sense of his own authority.

"Hell," he said, "if you go, Hinton, I'll put through a generous per diem for you and hazardous duty pay on top of that."

Still Ladislaw debated, trying to overcome years

of sedentary and safe routine. Finally he sighed a long, fluming sigh and nodded his head.

"I still fear it's too late," he told them. "Lord, I hope not, but mountain fever does its work quick. Quicker'n scat. If you get the medicine too late, you're gone beaver. But this young buck is right, I took an oath. If I say no, like I sure's hell want to, I guess I won't rightly get any sleep tonight nor deserve it. Saddle that mare, young Thomas. I'll go get my bag"

Chapter Ten

At first Honey Eater felt a terrible, unrelenting heat and a thirst so powerful it ached through her entire body. But then, gradually, like pain easing away under a soothing poultice, Honey Eater lost herself in the dream.

She was waiting alone in a secret, fragrant bower of willows well hidden from camp. The wind was a gentle kiss on her face; it blew tendrils of her long black hair back across her temples like soft wing tips. She wore her new blue calico dress. She had just bathed in the nearby river, and the soft dress clung to her like a second skin. It traced the dimpled swells of her nipples, the long, sweeping dip of her hips.

At first she was all alone and softly crying. But then, with the sudden and unexplained reality of dreams, Touch the Sky was beside her. His muscles felt hard, but his hold on her was gentle. She felt his lips tracing a hot, needful line from her lips, down her neck, into the front of her open dress. Then she felt an incredible, warm, wet pleasure ease over her nipples as he slid first one, then the other, into his eager mouth.

But then something was wrong. Just as something was always wrong for her and Touch the Sky. Before the horrible fever squeezed her in its death grip yet again, she realized this was no dream, but a real memory. They had met that way once before and held each other after she boldly declared to him that she considered herself his wife and would lie with him if he sent for her.

But as always when they stole time together, danger had reared its familiar head before their bodies could find the blissful release each sought in the other. Black Elk was coming along the bank, looking for her!

There was no bliss—only this burning hurt, even worse than the tortures of the blazing Staked Plain, where she had been the prisoner of Comanches and Kiowas. And the voice, gentle and sad, at the back of her awareness. The voice of her mother, Singing Woman, who was cut down by Pawnees before Honey Eater's eyes.

"You must remember to sing your death song soon, little daughter, or you will never cross over in peace."

Death Camp

*   *   *

Sharp Nosed Woman had not felt so sad inside her chest since the terrible attack that killed her brave Smiles Plenty. Looking at Honey Eater, seeing that momentary smile suddenly twisted in a paroxysm of fever pain, made her realize it was too late. The beautiful daughter of the proud Chief Yellow Bear was about to join her father and mother in the Land of Ghosts.

It was too late, too, too late. Neither Touch the Sky nor Black Elk had been able to defeat this grim champion of death, this warrior called mountain fever who needs no bullets to kill. Both Honey Eater and her little niece Laughing Brook had broken out in the faint rash, both had begun the final, desperate panting. It was this terrible dehydration that would kill them. If given water, they would lose twice as much from violent vomiting. All Sharp Nosed Woman could do was bathe them with cool cloths.

"Two pretty little flowers," she whispered, looking at the withered columbine petals in their hair.

Behind her, a baby cried piteously, a steady, hopeless puling. It was so terribly sad that even some brave warriors had tears in their eyes as they stopped and joined the chant groups outside the pest lodge. Night and day, without pause, these groups sang the ancient cure songs given to the people by Maiyun and the high holy ones.

For a moment Sharp Nosed Woman crossed to the entrance and glanced across the camp clearing. Her tired brow wrinkled with weary, disgusted anger as she glanced at Medicine Flute's tipi. The sly young brave, and his champion Wolf Who Hunts Smiling, made much of his shamanic powers and his supposed loyalty to his tribe. Yet the skinny, lazy, cowardly little weasel sat well away from the danger, blowing on that stupid bone flute. He claimed he was curing the sick ones, and he had made it clear that, if the cure failed, it was only because of the white man's stink clinging to Touch the Sky.

Medicine Flute was clever, she thought. His pronouncements were always such that he could claim credit when magic worked and blame Touch the Sky when it failed. But her anger was short-lived. It cost too much effort. And all this death and dying had made her far too weary for any needless effort.

She glanced back at Honey Eater, at the girl lying next to her. Best to sew their new moccasins, she told herself, so they'll be ready for their final journey.

"Are you surprised, cousin?" Wolf Who Hunts Smiling said bitterly. "These white skins are his old childhood friends. He drinks strong water with them, hides messages in trees for them, and in many other ways plays their dog. Can we truly be surprised that they would help the one called White Man Runs Him?"

The two braves and Swift Canoe sat their ponies

in the lee of a sandstone butte overlooking Fort Bates. Stone Mountain had been killed in the skirmish with the soldiers. Below, they watched Touch the Sky and his companions ride out on fresh, strong cavalry mounts. The paleface with them, who looked as if he had already been scalped once, must be the white-skin medicine man.

"There is nothing else for it now," Black Elk said grimly. His black eyes burned with murderous rage. "I do not care that there are only three of us now. With ammunition, I would attack them alone. But we are out of bullets, down to only a few arrows thanks to those bluecoats Woman Face led to us. We cannot mount another strike now."

"No," Wolf Who Hunts Smiling said, "not a full strike. But we can still make their life a hurting place."

Black Elk nodded. Exhaustion and determination combined to make him look as fierce as Wolf Who Hunts Smiling had ever seen him. He scowled so often that deep frown lines were etched into the cured leather of his face. Thick alkali dust coated his braid, his detached ear hung like a door falling off a white-skin lodge.

"Nothing of can," he told his cousin. "We will make their life a hurting place. I have been humiliated enough by Woman Face. I will not let him return with that white skin and his medicine."

Judd Cole

This threat secretly thrilled Wolf Who Hunts Smiling. Black Elk's hatred for Touch the Sky, like his own, had finally grown so all consuming that he would even let fellow Cheyennes die rather than allow that tall, pretend Cheyenne to best him!

"I have ears for this, Black Elk! What about me? Do you know what it has been like for me, stripped of my coup feathers by an act of the headmen? White Man Runs Him cost me the right to show others my battle record! Our Sioux cousins visit and sneer at me when they see I have not once counted coup. I, whose coup feathers nearly reached the ground like yours."

"As you say, cousin. We will not let him humiliate us again!"

Swift Canoe had been listening to this with a puzzled frown. "Brothers," he said slowly, "I hate him as do both of you. He killed my only brother with his cowardly treachery! But is this thing right, this letting our people die so that—"

"I have no ears for this womanly softness," Wolf Who Hunts Smiling snapped. "He who would be a leader of men cannot shirk back from hard duty."

He looked at his older cousin and held his eye, steadying Black Elk's resolve. "As you say, war leader, we cannot stop Woman Face and his companions. But we can kill that skinny, hairless white man. Without him, his medicine is useless."

120

"You say Ladislaw is with them?" Seth Carlson demanded.

"Yes, sir," the scout named MacGruder said. "Old Quinine himself. I saw his bony ass bumping up and down on that little mare Capt. Riley refused to sell you."

"Riley!" Carlson spat the word out with disgust, as if it tasted bitter on his tongue. "I should've know that Indian-loving bastard would mix in this. Prob'ly used his influence with the old man. That hick rail splitter hasn't even been to West Point, and Col. Neusbaum thinks he's a top hand."

MacGruder wisely held his counsel. Like most of the enlisted men, he knew that no officer at the fort would ever call Tom Riley a bastard to his face. Nor would any enlisted man call him that behind his back. Riley had been appointed from the ranks; he was not an elitist and a petty martinet like Carlson. Also unlike Carlson, Riley never touched a bite of food until he knew all of his men were eating. In the same spirit of warrior camaraderie, he never issued any order he wouldn't be willing to follow himself. As a result, his men would follow him into hell carrying empty carbines.

Hanchon's brazen move in forcing Carlson to halt the attack on the stagecoach had left the officer dangerously quiet. When he swore at his men and roweled his horse and threw his hat to the ground, he was mad. But when he clammed up as he was doing now, the men stood by for one hell of a blast. In one of these tempers, he had suddenly gone insane and beaten a stubborn pack mule to death with a trace chain.

For a long time Carlson squatted beside Beaver Creek, brooding. His company was bivouacked along the grassy bank. Shelter halves and dog tents were grouped by squads, carbines stood upright in groups of five at stack arms. The men were enjoying this duty. They had a tacit understanding with their commander. They kept their mouths shut while he broke every regulation in the operations manual; they, in turn, were permitted to slack off whenever possible. While Carlson steamed and fretted, they had thrown trotlines across the creek. Now the smell of fresh trout and bass frying filled the camp.

"All right," he finally said, making up his mind, "they've got to pass Lookout Bluff again on their way back to the Powder country, right?"

MacGruder nodded. "If they're in a hurry like you say, sir. They could cross farther upriver on the Shoshone, but that adds a half day's travel."

"No danger there. They'll ford at Crying Horse Bend."

Carlson paused, remembering a Blackfoot hunting party he had once obliterated in the Bear Paw Mountains with special weapons. It was true that Gatlings and such were virtually useless if Indians knew you had them. The Indians weren't fool enough to obligingly ride in front of the guns for you. But if they were caught by surprise, the dying would be over faster than a hungry man could gobble a biscuit.

"The new spur line from the fort is finished," he told the scout. "We're authorized for special munitions for these field maneuvers. The recruits haven't had their familiarization fire yet. I'm going to give you a requisition for the armory. Then I want you to oversee the loading."

"Of what, sir?"

Carlson smiled and stood up, swiping at some dust on his blue kersey trousers. He stretched his stiff back until it popped.

"Gatlings and Parrot artillery rifles," he finally replied. "This time we're going to blow those flea-bitten blanket asses off the face of the earth."

Tom Riley had a scout out too. But the man wasn't keeping track of the Indians. He was watching Seth Carlson's movements. Touch the Sky had warned Riley of the attack at Lookout Bluff. And since Carlson hadn't returned from maneuvers yet, it was a cinch bet he had more grief in store for Touch the Sky.

Despite his decision to help, Col. Neusbaum had drawn the line when Riley asked if a detachment could be sent with Ladislaw and the Indians. The most recent treaty signed at Fort Laramie strictly forbade him from risking his men in a potentially hostile movement without higher authorization. There was no time for that anyway, Riley knew.

As he turned the haggard-looking Indian ponies over to the private in charge of the graze guard, he made up his mind. "Thompson, graze these ponies with the rest and make sure they get a double ration of grain tonight. But before you do that, ride up to the stables and search out Cpl. Moats. Tell him to pick ten of his best sharpshooters and draw a few days' field rations. Then he's to stand by at the stables until I get there."

"Yes, sir!" The private saluted and turned, running toward his mount picketed nearby.

"Trooper!"

Thompson stopped and turned back around. "Sir!"

"Tell Cpl. Moats each man is to clean his weapon well and have thirty cartridges crimped and ready."

Chapter Eleven

By now Touch the Sky and his Cheyenne companions had been pushing themselves on sheer will alone. They had not slept since they'd left their Powder River camp, nor had they eaten anything more substantial than the pemmican in their legging sashes. They had not wasted even enough time to shoot and cook a few rabbits.

Their exhaustion showed in a certain dull glaze over their eyes. Like their enemy Wolf Who Hunts Smiling, their eyes shifted constantly on the alert for the ever expected attack. They rode in a four-point diamond formation—Touch the Sky at the fore, Little Horse to the rear, Tangle Hair and Two Twists riding the flanks. Ladislaw rode in the middle, as protected as a man could be when death lurked everywhere like a dry-gulcher.

It had not taken Ladislaw long to realize exactly how dangerous this mission really was. He knew those braves weren't protecting him out of courtesy. He had learned enough to know that he was caught up in some barbaric tribal power struggle. Time and again, despite the warm sun, he shivered inwardly as he pictured the two Indian factions dividing him in half like King Solomon axing that child in two.

Ladislaw had already made himself useful by disinfecting and bandaging Two Twists' wound. Now the contract surgeon chucked up his horse and moved up beside the tall Cheyenne leader.

"No need to give me the evil eye," Ladislaw groused, partly as a cover for his jitters. "I'll go back to my spot. Just want to suggest something."

"You're the doctor," Touch the Sky said with no trace of humor in his face.

"That's right, I am. And a good one, too, though these shit-for-brains malingerers at Fort Bates are too stupid to know it. They call me Sugar Pills and Old Quinine. But it doesn't need a doctor to see that you and your friends are getting sleep simple. You keep this up, one of you is going to make a serious mistake. Each of you swallow two of these."

Touch the Sky's glazed eyes dropped to the dark gleaming pills in Ladislaw's outstretched palm.

"What are they?"

"The soldiers call 'em Night Owls. Basically, each pill is the equivalent of drinking two cups of strong cowboy coffee, the kind that can float a nail and raise a blood blister on saddle leather. Soldiers on night picket take them, and settlers in wagon trains give 'em to the little children out on the plains. The littlest ones get so bored in that emptiness they pass out, fall off the bone shakers, and get crushed under the wheels."

When Touch the Sky hesitated, Ladislaw said, "Fine. You're the one said you're in a hurry, said you got loved ones to save. I'm just trying to help."

"Thanks."

Touch the Sky took the pills and signaled to the rest. All four braves swallowed the pills, grimacing.

"If this is how white soldiers eat, "Two Twists said, "I would rather eat horse droppings."

But soon Touch the Sky did feel more alert, and he could see that his friends did too. And just in time, for now they had ridden into perfect ambush country: a series of rolling hills covered with clumps of pine trees and hawthorn bushes.

At every moment Touch the Sky expected to take his last breath as a bullet found his lights. Sweat beaded along his scalp and rolled down his nape with a tickling sensation like lice digging at him. If was not merely the thought of death that gnawed at him. He wore that familiar fear like a pair of old moccasins. But he was intensely afraid of failure—the failure to get Ladislaw and the medicine back to camp in time.

Again he glanced all around, squinting against

the advancing sun. His eyes traversed the hills, scoured the trees, and delved deep into defiles and coulees. Now and then, after searching a sector normally, he would turn his head and study the same area from the corners of his eyes. Arrow Keeper had once showed him how peripheral vision could pick up some movements that straight-on vision often missed.

But at least they made fair, if not rapid, time on the cavalry mounts. The Cheyennes were not accustomed to such heavy and elaborate saddles, yet they could not dispense with them for fear of making the horses rebel. It was bad enough that these horses were not used to the smell of Indians. They obeyed well enough, being hard broken by the cruel methods of the whites but they were nervous and skittish. As for the Indians, they cringed inwardly as they thought about the iron bits white men shoved in a horse's mouth to control the animal. But urgency called for strong, well-trained mounts, and they had them. Unfortunately, the horses were trained for endurance, not speed. It was doubtful they could outrun Black Elk's band in a dead race, even though the Cheyenne ponies had seen brutal riding.

Touch the Sky was leading the little party up a long rise when, all in a moment, someone leapt at him from behind a boulder. He swung hard in the saddle, his feet caught clumsily in the stirrups, and brought his Sharps .45-120 up to the ready. His finger curled inside the trigger guard.

Death Camp

Then the heat of shame came into his face when he realized the figure had only been his own shadow suddenly catching his eye on the gray face of the sunlit rock. Perhaps he had trained his side vision a bit too well if it was going to turn him into a nervous girl who started at every owl hoot.

Luckily, no one had seen him nearly shoot his own shadow point-blank. Despite the Night Owl pills, he saw that he was clearly still nerve frazzled from exhaustion and worry. He must get control of himself and settle down. He was a leader. In a sense his entire tribe was behind him right now, pushing him on even as they needed him to pull them to safety. He could not give in now. If he was hurting, what was it like for Honey Eater and the rest?

That last thought focused him like a hard slap to the face. No more of this jumping at shadows. He turned in the saddle to check the progress of the others, and he was just in time to see an arrow zwip past Ladislaw's nose, missing his head by a hairbreadth.

"Brothers!" Touch the Sky bellowed. "Look hard to your flanks and shoot for vitals! Our enemies are upon us!"

The arrow had thwacked into a tree so hard that the shaft still vibrated when Touch the Sky reached the ashen-faced doctor.

"I know you're a healer and not a fighter. But even the gentle beaver reacts to danger! Don't sit your horse, catching flies with your mouth, when you're being shot at!" Touch the Sky told him. "Either spur your mount or dismount and take cover. If you sit still, you're just helping your killer adjust his aim after the first miss."

"Spur my mount?" Ladislaw said in a voice made tight with fear. "Lad, you and I live in two different worlds. While you're dodging bullets and arrows, I'm usually soaking my feet in Epsom salts and reading poetry. Spur my mount? Cheyenne, that damn arrow nicked my nose! It's all I can do right now to keep from pissing myself!"

Little Horse had moved in close with his shotgun ready, all four revolving barrels loaded with buckshot for close-in killing. Two Twists and Tangle Hair, meantime, had boldly rushed a nearby ridge. Touch the Sky could hear the sound of unshod hoofs retreating behind the ridge. There would be no more attempts for now—not from Black Elk's band anyway. This arrow meant one good piece of news: His enemies must be out of bullets.

But where, he thought nervously as he craned his neck to glance all around them, was Seth Carlson?

"That's the last gun emplacement, sir," Sgt. Nolan Reece reported proudly. "Supervised 'em myself. We got the entire draw below covered for saturation fire. A titmouse couldn't slip through there."

Seth Carlson dropped into a squat behind the

Gatling. It had been unhooked from its clumsy wooden carriage and mounted in a sturdy base of rocks and dirt. Its notched sight overlooked the Old Sioux Trace as it wound past the steep headland of Lookout Bluff.

"The other Gatling is set up over yonder at the southern approach," Reece said, pointing.

"Who's firing it?"

Cpl. James, sir. I got Pvt. Lanier feeding rounds into the hopper."

"Good." Carlson approved this strategy with a nod. "They did a good job on the Blackfoot camp."

"That James is a Kentucky boy, sir. Them ol' boys don't bother with this fancy-ass scientific shooting. They lick their thumbs to get their windage, and then they just peddle it to 'em."

Carlson was in a touchy mood and simply dismissed Reece's needless talk with an impatient wave of one hand. "What about the Parrots? You space 'em out even like I said?"

"For a fact, sir. Paced it off myself. Six artillery pieces about fifty feet apart." Reece rubbed a knuckle across his teamster's mustache.

"Whoever rides through below has got to get past two Gatlings firing three hundred fifty rounds a minute, six artillery rifles throwing twenty-pound exploding shells, and a few dozen sharpshooters with full bandoliers. It's gunna be hotter'n the hinges of hell down there. Couldn't a pissant slip through that draw."

Carlson did not look so convinced. "I'd agree,"

he said, "if it was anyone but Hanchon. I'm starting to wonder if his life is charmed."

"Ah, all due respect to your rank, sir. But that's what they say about that blanket-assed Apache Geronimo too. But if his red ass is so charmed, how come he always hauls it deep into Mexico so's he can cover it good? Hanchon ain't charmed; he's just been uncommon lucky."

"That he has," Carlson said. Reece was often irritating, but he had hit on a home truth here, and Carlson found his opinion encouraging.

A trooper on lookout near the southern approach trotted closer and saluted Carlson. "Sir! We got us a herd of elk heading this way hell-bent for election. They'll be pushin' through the draw in a few minutes."

"Could have a couple of the men shoot us some fresh meat," Reece said. "The troopers're tired of desecrated beef."

Knowing Reece meant the new desiccated meat rations issued to soldiers in the field, Carlson nodded. Then his big, bluff, sunburned face split in a slight grin as he thought of something else.

"Sergeant, have the men fired the new guns for battle sights?"

"Battle sights?" Reece grinned as he caught his superior's drift. "No, sir, they have not, for a fact."

"All right. Have them load and then stand by to fire."

"Right, sir!"

Reece relayed the order to the gun crews while

Carlson walked the length of the bluff, returning to the Gatling gun that marked the first emplacement in this deadly gauntlet. He tilted the black brim of his hat to cut the glare of the westering sun. Then, below, he spotted the small herd. Perhaps a hundred head, racing at full speed and raising dust puffs as they approached.

"Listen up!" Carlson shouted. "I want every swinging peeder in this man's outfit showing me how to shoot! Let's see who's got the biggest pair on him. We're going to turn those elks into stew meat. Think of them as that much less for the savages to eat so they can go on killing soldiers.

"But wait for my command before you open fire. I want them killed after they enter the draw. That way the Indians won't see the dead animals until it's too late."

The men whooped and grinned. They welcomed this bit of sport to break up the monotony up here on the bluff. The fishing had been first-rate at Beaver Creek, the shade cool and inviting. Up here a man could only sweat and slap at gnats.

Rounds were stuffed into the magazine hoppers of the Gatlings. Elongated, fin-tailed rockets were dropped into the rifled bores of the big Parrot guns. The riflemen crammed rounds through the butt plates of their carbines. The herd thundered closer.

Carlson moved down the line and shouted, "Ready on the right?"

"All ready on the right!" Reece said.

"Ready on the left?"

"All ready on the left!"

"All ready on the right, all ready on the left. All ready on the firing line. Watch your targets. Targets!"

The Parrots kicked back hard and belched smoke and flames. The Gatlings chattered and bucked. The precision carbines cracked with the solid report of good tooling. Below, great chunks of earth and rock and bloody elk intermingled as they flew high into the air. The herd never had a chance. Those not killed by the artillery shells fell under a wall of bullets.

"Cease fire!" Carlson bellowed when the last animal lay twitching in its own gore, dead but still nerved for motion.

A cheer flew up from the men. Reece flashed an ear-to-ear smile. "Holy Hannah, Cap'n! If them woulda been Injuns, it'd be raining feathers in Laramie right now!"

It wasn't Indians. But Carlson couldn't help sharing a grin with his platoon sergeant. It had indeed been an impressive slaughter.

"No, sir," Reece said. "A pissant couldn't slip through that trap."

The ride was hard and dangerous, and no amount of pills could defeat the exhaustion threatening to overwhelm Touch the Sky and his Cheyenne companions.

Soon enough they would reach Lookout Bluff.

Death Camp

Since he had no idea where Carlson was, Touch the Sky knew he should expect trouble there. But for now Black Elk's band was again worrying him. Enough time had elapsed since their last attempt on Ladislaw. By now they must have a new scheme in hand.

Once again Ladislaw was riding in the center of a four-point diamond formation. They stopped briefly at a runoff rill so the horses could drink. Touch the Sky could not remember being this tired since his vision quest to Medicine Lake when enemies closed in from every quarter and sleep was impossible. The situation was similar now. Only this time it wasn't just his life that hung in the balance.

He dismounted, threw the horse's bridle, and watched the animal stretch its long neck out to drink from the little streamlet. Everything was a blur, as if his tired eyes saw things underwater. For a moment, just a blessed moment as the horse drank, the tired Cheyenne let his head fall forward and closed his eyes.

When he opened his eyes again, a shock wave of fear slammed into him. Dr. Ladislaw had wandered well away from cover to relieve himself, and none of the others had yet noticed him.

Touch the Sky shouted a warning even as Little Horse looked up and also spotted the danger. Both of them started forward with the swiftness of charging cats, closing the distance between them and Ladislaw. Touch the Sky steeled his muscles for the jump, then saw Wolf Who Hunts Smiling stepping from behind a deadfall, an arrow notched in his bow.

Touch the Sky leapt at the same moment Little Horse did. They crashed down onto Ladislaw and toppled him. But they were an eyeblink too late to completely avoid the deadly arrow—as Touch the Sky landed on the doctor, he felt a pain like white-hot fire rip into his back.

Chapter Twelve

"I know it hurts like hell," Ladislaw said. "But it missed all the important places. You're just gonna feel stiff for a while."

Touch the Sky nodded, grimacing against the pain. He was sprawled out facedown on the ground. "I've had arrows in me before," he said. "Just push the tip through quick. We're losing more time."

He gritted his teeth against the anticipated pain. But Ladislaw shook his head. "Can't poke it through."

"Why not?"

"The tip is made out of tin."

At these words, Touch the Sky's expression alerted his companions. He translated this news for them. Nothing was more deadly than an arrow tip made from white man's tin. Once in the body, it bent easily and clinched to bone. Instead of sliding out easily, like chipped flints and stone points, the tin became a deadly blade inside, tearing and gouging and severing vital arteries.

"You said it wasn't bad!"

"It's not, right now. It's in a great spot. But it'll play hell on you if I just poke her through. Might even make you bleed to death."

"Then go," Touch the Sky said desperately. "Get back to camp now. There's no time for fancy surgery on me."

"Never mind fancy surgery," Ladislaw muttered, snapping open his kit. "I told you I'm a damn good doctor. I invented a little something for these injuries. We'll be in the saddle in ten minutes."

He pulled a length of oddly looped wire out of the leather kit. "The problem with these tin points is how they're deliberately tied loose to the shaft. That way it breaks off inside. You have to loop the whole thing and just lift it out following the entrance wound. You do that"—he paused, squinting as he lowered his homemade instrument into the jagged tear—"and you're in business." As he pulled the point out and proudly displayed it to the others, Little Horse grinned in amazement, as did his two companions.

"Whoa!" Ladislaw protested when Touch the Sky started to rise. "Stay there just a minute while

Death Camp

I rinse the wound with disinfectant. Then we can ride."

Touch the Sky winced when the alcohol was splashed onto his injury. But it was a small ordeal, indeed, and blessedly brief. Ladislaw was right—he was stiff. Still, very soon they were riding north again, approaching the huge headland of Lookout Bluff.

"Brother," Little Horse said, "do your thoughts fly with mine?"

They were riding side by side, staring up at the prominent land mass. Sister Sun was slowly dropping toward her resting place in the west. But enough light remained to make them good targets.

"If your thoughts are bloody and colored Soldier Blue," Touch the Sky said, "then, yes, buck, mine fly with yours."

"What is there for it? As you say, we have no time for scouting. Some kind of trap is waiting for us. Do we risk it and take our losses?"

Touch the Sky glanced back toward Ladislaw. "Our losses could be accepted. But there is one loss we cannot risk."

"Straight words, buck. What, then?"

"They are up there," Touch the Sky said. "They must be. We cannot afford to wait until darkness falls and attempt to elude them again. What did we do when we needed to sneak past Pawnee sentries and save our village?"

Little Horse grinned. "We created a diversion."

"We did, buck, and we shall again. You know

that horses cannot ride past on the west side of the bluff?"

Little Horse nodded. "Even more scree has fallen back there than lies in the pass around front. A mule could not easily manage it."

"No, so of course they will not be looking for us to use that route. But what if one of us went back there—one of us with shotgun shells full of black powder? What if there was a loud explosion, war whoops, and arrows flying up over the brim onto the soldiers from the back?"

"They would think," Little Horse said slowly, "that an attack was being mounted from that side, that a war party was ascending. Then they would rush in that direction to defend themselves."

Touch the Sky nodded. "They would. Then the remaining braves would have to make a rush for it to get past. The lone brave would be on his own. He would have to fend for himself and get back to camp on his own."

Like Touch the Sky, Little Horse knew the plan was an extreme long shot. But also like Touch the Sky, he realized there was no other option. Little Horse had sniffed the wind again, and he smelled the strong presence of many cavalry mounts—far more than the few they presently rode. Carlson and his Indian Killers were waiting for the braves.

"We both know that I will be the lone brave," Little Horse said. "Be ready to make your move when you hear the attack begin."

"Take Tangle Hair too, so there will be more

racket and shooting. Be careful getting into position," Touch the Sky warned him. "If they spot you and we lose the element of surprise, we will all be feeding the worms."

Even as more time passed, making Touch the Sky chafe at the delay, he had no regrets about this decision. Despite any concrete evidence, he was utterly convinced a powerful attack force lay in wait for them.

He had carefully explained the plan to Two Twists and Ladislaw. Two Twists had not even blinked an eye; Ladislaw, in contrast, lost all the color in his face and fell silent. But Touch the Sky watched the sedentary, timid man nerve himself for this dangerous move. And the Cheyenne realized that he and his comrades were used to danger; indeed, it was the ridge they lived on. For Ladislaw, this was a real effort of bravery. He was even more admirable for remaining so stoic and determined in the face of his fear. The three of them had taken cover in a cutbank well back from the shadow of the bluff.

"Be ready," Touch the Sky said in a voice just above a whisper. "Little Horse should be making his move soon. We must take advantage of the very first moments after he detonates his powder, when the white skins are likely to panic and leave their positions to check behind them."

But as things turned out, it was Touch the Sky's horse, not his friend, who triggered the desperate break. And not when it was supposed to happen. Busy listening for the explosion from behind the bluff, Touch the Sky failed, at first, to notice the angry, buzzing rattle when his horse moved forward a little. He noticed it just in time to yank his own mount around and out of danger. But Ladislaw's mare, with all the medicine on her back, suddenly spooked and jerked away from the contract surgeon before he could secure his grip on her reins. In numb horror, Touch the Sky watched the mare break toward the narrowing draw below the bluff.

In seconds the animal would break into a withering field of fire. The death of a horse could mean the end of this mission. How would they get that medicine once the horse went down in sight of the soldiers' weapons?

All these thoughts flew through Touch the Sky's head in the space of an eyeblink. So did another: the thought of the magic bloodstone in his parfleche. Arrow Keeper had left the stone when he parted from the tribe to build his death wickiup. The old shaman swore the stone, when empowered by sacred words and faith in the supernatural, could make the holder invisible to his enemies. Desperately, Touch the Sky lunged at the horse as it flew past and managed to grip the saddle horn and cantle. His muscles straining like taut cables, he threw himself onto the panicked mount.

They were only seconds away from a clear field of fire. He dug the stone out of his parfleche, gripped it hard, then quickly and fervently sought

Death Camp

Maiyun's help, not for himself, but for the people.

He heard the sudden shout from above, a hateful voice he recognized all too well: "Here they come! Put at 'em!" Then the panicked mount broke into the open, and Touch the Sky braced himself for death.

"Here they come!" Seth Carlson shouted. "Put at 'em!"

Eagerly, he rushed to the brim and stared down, ready to direct the artillery and Gatling fire. He could hear the charging horse, its hoofclops as clear as hail on a tin roof. Hoping for the first shot at Hanchon, Carlson had eased his finger inside the trigger guard and taken up the slack. But staring below with his face frozen in eager expectation, he slowly took his carbine out of his shoulder socket and stared harder below.

What the hell? There was plenty of light yet—at least an hour's worth. And he could hear a horse down there as plain as anything. So where in the hell was it?

"Reece?"

"Sir!"

"You see anything?"

"My hand to God, sir, there ain't a damn thing down there."

Suddenly, an explosion behind them made Carlson flinch and almost drop his carbine. The explosion was followed by hideous Cheyenne war whoops, then a few arrows flew straight up and clattered down onto them.

"We're being attacked from the rear!" Sgt. Reece bellowed. "Reverse positions or they'll cut us down!"

"Wait!" Carlson screamed. "Delay that command! It's some kind of damn trick. It's a feint!"

But it was too late. His men, convinced they were about to be overrun by scalp-crazy savages, hurried to the opposite side of the bluff to counter this new threat.

The first part was over before Touch the Sky could even believe he was still alive. The cavalry horse had bolted straight through the draw. Once Touch the Sky had glanced overhead and spotted Carlson. The befuddled officer was staring right at him, yet failed to shoot. And miraculously, he was safe on the other side of the drainage gully, out of the line of fire.

As the din began from the back of the bluff, Touch the Sky frantically signaled to Two Twists and Ladislaw. While the soldiers were distracted, the other two made their break. Ladislaw rode Touch the Sky's pony. His face was as white as new snow by the time he joined the tall Cheyenne on the other side.

"Now fly like the wind!" Touch the Sky told them. "We must make the river before they can catch us!"

But it was already too late. Carlson, never having bought the ruse anyway, had corralled a few gunners and returned to the east brim of the bluff. Now he spotted his enemies, and though they were out of effective rifle range, the Parrots could still play hell with them. The first rockets lobbed in, and suddenly the earth was exploding all around Touch the Sky and his companions.

The horses panicked as dirt and debris rained all over them. Fighting for control cost the little party even more time. Now the soldiers were racing down to form an attack force below the bluff.

The plan had come close to working. But as Touch the Sky savagely fought to control the recalcitrant cavalry mount, he realized with a sinking feeling that they were losing their slim margin of safety. How could they outrun their enemy without enough lead? But, faintly at first, then louder, came the rousing bugle notes of *Boots and Saddles*.

He glanced behind them and saw a squad of soldiers racing toward the bluff at a gallop, and they weren't shooting at the Cheyennes. They were directing their fire onto the bluff!

A grin tugged at Touch the Sky's lips as he realized Tom Riley was once again riding to the aid of his Cheyenne friend. He knew Riley would detain Carlson so the Cheyennes could escape. But even as he got his horse under control and led his friends toward the river, he couldn't help wondering if their efforts were all for nothing. Had too much time passed? Were Honey Eater and the rest already dead?

Chapter Thirteen

"Gather near me, little ones," cried the old grandfather, "and hear the story about Mouse Road, the great warrior. When the battle was finally almost over, all of Mouse Road's Cheyenne brothers lay dead. But Mouse Road had fought with such skill and courage that his Crow enemies sent a word bringer to his rifle pit.

" 'We will not kill you," they said, "for you are a brave and honorable man, a worthy enemy. In you we see the same traits we admire in our men. We will draw off now while you ride away in peace. Go, brave one.'

" ' I will not thank you for your praise, 'Mouse Road replied, 'for your words are only truth and I have earned them. I also trust your word. But there around me lie my comrades, dead as stones.

146

Death Camp

I trained for war with them, learned the secrets of the hunt with them and bounced their children on my knee. How will I return to my village without them? Why would I want to? Come and finish this sport. I am for you!'

"And three more enemies were sent under that day before the last Cheyenne brave was slain. . . . "

With a guilty start, Sharp Nosed Woman woke from her dream. The exhausted woman had nodded out for a moment. Now she crossed to Honey Eater and lay her hand on the girl's forehead.

"Maiyun help us!" Sharp Nosed Woman pulled her hand back as if the touch had burned her, and in fact it had burned her. For an instant it felt as if she had plunged her hand into glowing embers.

More deaths, more dying, more suffering, more grief—when would it end? Only when the last of them had died? Fortunately, the tribe's quick work in tracing the source of the infection had allowed them to quickly isolate the sick and infected. But even so, more than 30 lay dying, with six others already crossed over.

The latest one to go into the final phase was little Laughing Brook. Her heartbeat was fainter than the pulse of a baby bird, and her normally flawless skin was splotchy from the fever raging inside her and thinning her blood dangerously.

"Maiyun help us," Sharped Nosed Woman said again.

But she knew that Maiyun, for His own inscrutable reasons, would not save them. Nor would that stupid, toneless music coming from Medicine Flute's bone instrument. More and more of the people had gathered around his tipi, hoping his medicine could help.

Sharp Nosed Woman believed it was too late for white man or red man's medicine. She no longer held out any hope for assistance from Touch the Sky or Black Elk. Indeed, perhaps the two jealous stags had locked horns in mortal combat even while their tribe lay dying. Men were that way, she thought, everything with them was always war, fighting, pride, and their sacred honor. Was life not hard enough? Why did they have to make it harder with their incessant fighting?

"No, little Honey Eater," she said, "this time your tall, strong brave cannot save you. But if any man might have, he is the man. Black Elk will not shed a tear for your loss. But this Touch the Sky? His is a love beyond all words to measure it. I fear the very grief from your passing may kill him or drive him to fall on his knife. I would gladly burn my beaded wedding shawl if it would mean he could touch your living hand only once more before you cross over."

Sharp Nosed Woman had spent the time, when she wasn't trying to uselessly comfort one of the sick, sewing new moccasins for Honey Eater and Laughing Brook. Both were in her clan, so it was proper to perform this final service. It would be she too who would wash and dress their bodies for the final journey to the Land of Ghosts.

Outside, the sad, monotonous chanting of the cure songs went on. The rhythmic sound comforted her, made her feel her link to the rest of the people during this terrible tragedy.

And clearly there was more suffering ahead. Since she had given up all hope, she just wanted the suffering to be over as quickly as possible. Indeed, it was customary among the Southern Cheyenne to smother young children who caught mountain fever.

Looking at the twisted masks of pain that had replaced Honey Eater and Laughing Brook's pretty faces, she was tempted to do the same. A few moments of weak struggling over each one of these poor sufferers would bring peace.

Just then, from the back of the crowded pest lodge, she heard a gurgling, gasping noise like a sucking chest wound: the death rattle of another infant choking in its own mucus and giving up the ghost. At least the child's pain was almost over.

Quickly, Sharp Nosed Woman rushed to the child's wicker cradle. The importance of this moment was holy, and even her exhaustion could not dull the love in her as she lay her hand on the babe's scalding head.

As the child measured out the final breath of its brief existence on earth, Sharp Nosed Woman sang the sad words of the Cheyenne death song:

Nothing lives long,
Only the earth and the mountains.

Tom Riley's squad of sharpshooters had arrived in the nick of time to ensure that Touch the Sky, Two Twists, and Dr. Ladislaw would face no more harassment from Seth Carlson. But Touch the Sky knew that, once again, he and the others would have to ford the dangerous Shoshone River at Crying Horse Bend. This would be especially difficult for the inexperienced Ladislaw. And what better time for Black Elk and Wolf Who Hunts Smiling to make their next deadly move?

At least the tall young warrior's mind was set easy on one point: the fate of Little Horse and Tangle Hair. Thanks to Riley's intervention, they were able to slip away and join their band again.

"Brothers," he told his three weary companions while their ponies drank from the last water hole before the Shoshone, "this should be the final leg of our journey—also the most treacherous. Black Elk will be desperate to save face before the tribe. He cannot let me best him again, as he sees it."

"Save face," Little Horse said bitterly. The constant pace of this mission had finally told on the sturdy little warrior. He no longer made jokes about death being merely one more pony to ride. "Save face, he calls it. As if a warrior's pride is more important than the life of his own good wife."

Exhaustion had made him careless. The moment Little Horse finished speaking these words, he regretted them—not for Black Elk's sake, but for Touch the Sky's. The last thing that worried and battered warrior needed was to be reminded of Honey Eater's danger—a danger that might well have become a death.

"Brother," Little Horse said, "I regret those careless words."

But Touch the Sky was not one to show whatever deep feelings they may have stirred up. Nor was he one to leave any friend feeling awkward in front of others.

"I regret them too, buck. Not because you spoke them, for no offense was intended or caused. But only because they are true. However, are we white men who discuss the various causes of the winds even while our people need us? Let us ride and swap our regrets over the firepit during the cold moons."

Since Ladislaw had learned his lesson, he stayed close to his Cheyenne protectors. They bore straight north toward the Shoshone, feeling a little safer as the ground cover thinned to a few dark clumps of juniper and a scrawny jackpine or two. But once again the cottonwood and willow thickets began to proliferate as they entered the broad tableland close to the river.

Touch the Sky's exhaustion had settled deep into his bone marrow. Huge, dark pockets filled the hollows under his eyes. But despite the bone-numbing weariness, he forced his mind to remain clear and sharp. They were approaching the river. He must come up with some kind of plan to help ensure their safe fording of the flood-swollen river. He would rely on his braves to help him.

When they crested the last ridge overlooking the river, Touch the Sky halted them. For a long moment, he studied the terrain on the opposite bank carefully: every bush, every tree, every cluster of boulders or up-thrusting ledge.

"Brothers," he said slowly, "let us assume that our tribal enemies are lurking at the river."

"A wise assumption," Tangle Hair said grimly.

"As you say, brother. Now, where would they strike?"

"Clearly, at Crying Horse Bend," Little Horse said. "Where else?"

"Yes," Touch the Sky said, eyes still scouring the river below. "But on which side?"

His words left his companions silent as they tried to catch his drift. Ladislaw watched their faces intently, not understanding a word but knowing this was important to the longevity of his white hide. Little Horse started to catch on. "We have, each of us, assumed that they shall have forded by now and will attack from the opposite bank. But the cover is much thicker on this side."

"Much," Tangle Hair said, grasping his meaning. "So they could leave their ponies much closer. Which they must do, for they plan to kill us and take the medicine and whiteskin shaman back with them."

Touch the Sky nodded encouragement. Thus the warriors thought aloud as one. "Now, if you were on this bank, where is the spot you would choose to leave your pony?"

"The nearest place," Two Twists said, "where they would be hidden, yet close to hand."

"Straight words, buck. A place such as that big deadfall just before the bend."

Slowly, the rest nodded, seeing how sensible all this was, and Touch the Sky said, "Either they are there or they are not. We will assume they are. If we are wrong, little will be lost because we are cautious. Tangle Hair!"

"I have ears, buck, and no thread in them like Black Elk."

"You have a stout heart too, warrior. The rest of us will swing to the east and approach the ford from an angle, diverting Black Elk's band from watching to the west where their ponies are probably hidden. You swing wide to the west and come up on that deadfall from the other side of the bend.

"They will make their move when we are in the water. At the first sign of trouble, leap into the open with their ponies' tethers in your hand. Fire your weapon to gain their attention; then wait long enough to let them start after you before you leave with their mounts. Ride hard and scatter them to the four directions, or bring them back to camp if you can."

It was a desperate plan, one based on scanty information and half-formed hunches. But all agreed it was at least a plan and the best they could hope for under the current time constraints.

Touch the Sky explained the strategy to Ladislaw in English.

"We got to cross that river?" he said, staring at the boiling, churning foam.

Touch the Sky nodded. "Unless you have pills that will grow wings on us."

As agreed, Tangle Hair dropped back behind the ridge. Staying below the crest, he angled off toward the deadfall. Meantime, staying conspicuously in the open, Touch the Sky led his small band down to the ford.

The cavalry horses showed more nervousness than the Indian ponies had. But the mounts were well trained for obedience. Rolling their eyes until they were all whites, they nonetheless bravely plunged into the raging water.

Ladislaw looked like a man about to walk the plank. Touch the Sky and Little Horse, constantly watching for attackers, kept him close between them as they splashed into the swirling waters. Two Twists waited behind them, his British trade rifle at the ready as he scoured the bank.

"Holy Hannah!" Ladislaw said as a geyser of foam soaked the front of his shirt.

"Hold on!" Touch the Sky shouted. "Hold on! If that current gets you, you're worm fodder!"

Despite their fear, the cavalry mounts were strong from regular graining. They held up well enough against the vicious pull of the current. But in their nervousness, the Cheyennes had failed to check the cinches on Ladislaw's saddlebag.

Death Camp

"Brother!" Little Horse shouted above the din of the raging river and the wild nickering of the horses.

Touch the Sky looked where Little Horse, wild-eyed with panic, was pointing. And then he spotted the saddlebag containing the medicine. The bag had just been ripped loose, and it was about to tumble out past them into the middle of the swift current!

Every muscle tense with instant desperation, Touch the Sky leapt off his struggling mount. He hit the ice-cold water, felt himself being sucked under, and struggled to the surface again. He swam hard, legs scissoring madly, trying to reach the floundering bag before it was swept under and away forever. Meantime, Little Horse had all he could do to keep Ladislaw in the saddle.

Touch the Sky groped, but missed. He tried again and just missed again. Then two figures stepped out from the thickets behind them. Suddenly, deadly arrows were flying into the river all around his head. Two Twists, frustrated, could see the arrows, but could spot no target from his position on the bank.

But Tangle Hair made his move, exactly as planned. He jumped into the open and fired his weapon to get the attention of Black Elk's band. Knowing they were ruined without mounts, Swift Canoe instantly gave chase. Tangle Hair tore off, heading the ponies by a single leadline.

This startling turn of events did indeed distract

their tribal enemies. And Two Twists had spotted Black Elk and Wolf Who Hunts Smiling. His trade rifle cracked over and over, forcing them to cover down while his companions finished the ford.

The saddlebag was inches from Touch the Sky's grasping fingers. It was on the verge of hitting the main current and floating away forever. He kicked, felt water rush into his lungs, and gasped for breath. Blindly, he struggled while his head was pulled inexorably under. He made one final grab and his fingers locked onto leather.

He was well downriver from the ford by the time he finally dragged himself ashore. But the dripping bag, medicine safe in its waterproofed vials, was in his hands. And his friends were safe—dripping like drowned rats, but safe.

"Brother," Little Horse said when he could speak again, "Tangle Hair has saved us! He stole their ponies, and there is no livestock anywhere in this area. We have finally turned Black Elk and his roosters into impotent capons!"

Touch the Sky nodded. Black Elk and Wolf Who Hunts Smiling were finally out of the picture. But now began the final desperate battle against the most terrible enemy of all: time.

Chapter Fourteen

Sharp Nosed Woman hardly cared when she heard the camp crier racing up and down the village streets, announcing the arrival of Touch the Sky and his band. What did it matter? This whiteskin medicine man they had in tow was too late, far too late. Sharp Nosed Woman knew the progress of mountain fever. Once the victims went into deep unconsciousness and the rapid, choking breathing started, death soon came on swift wings to claim them. And every last one of them had reached that stage. It was dawn of the third sleep since they were stricken—far too late.

Weary, glad the suffering was nearly over, she crossed to the entrance and lifted the hide flap. There, about to raise the flap, stood Touch the Sky. His face was an agony of uncertainty. A nervous-looking white man accompanied him.

"You are too late," she said to Touch the Sky, and Ladislaw got an instant translation by watching the young buck's tortured face.

It was as if he had been struck a fatal blow, which, nonetheless, left him standing, waiting to topple. "She is gone?" he whispered, unable to find voice for the words.

After Ladislaw hurried inside, Sharp Nosed Woman said, "Not yet, but any moment now. They are all past help."

The warrior started to step inside, but Ladislaw's sharp command cut through the fog of his grief and worry. "Don't come in here! They aren't contagious in the initial stages, but all of these poor souls surely are contagious now. I've had the vaccine; you haven't. It's not just your own safety. You'll give it to the rest in your tribe."

Ladislaw stopped briefly beside each patient, then sighed, shook his head, and stood up. He looked at Touch the Sky and shrugged helplessly. "They're too far gone. Way too far, all of them. Their souls belong to the Creator now."

His words pierced Touch the Sky with the force of bullets. From where he stood, gripping the hide entrance flap, he could see the inconspicuous mound where Honey Eater lay in her robes. Ladislaw closed his bag and mopped at his sweaty pate with a handkerchief.

"I'm awfully sorry, young fella," he said sincerely. "Lord knows you done your best. You got us here as quick as you could under the circumstances."

"There's nothing you can do?"

Ladislaw shook his head. "We're about eight hours too late for the best among them—maybe a whole day late for the sickest. It's hopeless."

Touch the Sky looked at Sharp Nosed Woman's weary, grief-ravaged face. She too had gone through a terrible ordeal, just as he had. Then he looked at Ladislaw, for he had just made up his mind.

"I want you to treat them anyway," he said. "Hopeless or not, treat them."

"You don't understand, son. They're—"

"I understand, Doctor. Treat them anyway."

"But—"

"Treat them anyway," Touch the Sky said. "Treat all of them, any with a breath still left in their nostrils."

"Son, what's the point, they—"

"Treat them!"

Touch the Sky's tone would brook no debate. Ladislaw shrugged, a shadow of worry passing over his face. Touch the Sky saw that worried look and understood. "Forget the stories you've heard about other tribes. You will not be killed if your medicine fails. I will not let you be touched, but treat them."

"It's blamed foolishness, but I'll do it. You might just as well go about your business instead of standing there gawking at me. Even if they had a chance, it would take the better part of a day for the medicine to work."

Touch the Sky dropped the flap and turned. Then he slowly and carefully wove his way through the mourners and chanters. From the corner of his eye, he saw Tangle Hair return to camp leading the ponies he'd stolen from Black Elk's band. But Touch the Sky failed to greet him because all of his attention was focused elsewhere. Little Horse, not liking the grim set of his friend's lips, fell into step behind him. At least, Little Horse consoled himself, neither Black Elk or Wolf Who Hunts Smiling was here, or blood would surely flow.

The knot of people who had gathered around Medicine Flute parted when Touch the Sky strode through them. Medicine Flute was about to sound yet another toneless note when Touch the Sky seized the leg-bone flute from his lips. A sharp crack sounded when Touch the Sky snapped it in half against his thigh. He pitched both broken halves off into the trees.

"You skinny, lazy coward," Touch the Sky said. "It is bad enough that you hide in your tipi while your brothers are on the warpath, that you eat a generous share of meat you never kill. It is bad enough that you play the conniving dog for Wolf Who Hunts Smiling and Black Elk and the rest of the Bull Whips. It is bad enough that you pretend to visions and shaman powers and thus not only mock the high holy ones but prey on the faith of the people.

"All this is serious enough. But while our people lie dying, you will not mock true shamanism and waste the prayer energy of all these believers. If I hear you blowing on another flute, I am going to string a new bow with your guts. Do you take the meaning of my words?"

Medicine Flute could put up an arrogant front when surrounded by his supporters. But he truly was a coward, especially when his chief allies were not at hand to lend him false courage. He merely dropped his lidded gaze from that of this stern warrior and said, "As you will. My medicine is strong enough to survive a broken flute."

"Your medicine, white liver, is even more faint than your manhood."

With that Touch the Sky walked off. He saw Ladislaw emerge from the pest lodge. Touch the Sky searched the doctor's face until Ladislaw nodded, assuring him he'd completed the treatment, hopeless though it seemed.

"Brother," Touch the Sky said to Little Horse, "feed the white skin and find a place for him to rest. Then go to your tipi, eat something, and rest yourself. Soon I will come to wake you up. I need your assistance."

Little Horse looked at him asquint. He did not like the look or feel of this. "Assistance in what, brother?"

"You will find out all in good time, buck. Now eat and rest."

Touch the Sky followed his own advice. He returned to his tipi, ate a handful of venison, then told the crier to wake him when the morning sun had traveled the width of four lodge poles. He fell into his robes and slept like a dead man until the crier shook him out.

Like a she-bear eating for her cubs, Touch the Sky forced himself to eat more venison when he awoke. For he knew he would need much strength to face the ordeal looming before him.

One last task remained before he roused Little Horse. Touch the Sky walked down the long, grassy slope to the river. A huge sweat lodge had been made by stretching hides over a frame of bent saplings. Touch the Sky stepped inside and built a fire to heat a circle of rocks. When they glowed red-hot, he filled a rawhide pail with river water, stripped naked, and stepped back inside to pour the cool water over the glowing rocks.

Instantly the lodge filled with billowing steam. For a long time Touch the Sky sat silent and still, letting the vapors rise all around him and permeate his pores. He cleared his mind of all thought, preparing himself for the ordeal ahead. Once again, as so many times before, the time was coming—the time when he would have to visualize his pain as a bright red ball and then place it outside of himself, as Arrow Keeper had taught him. Only thus could a man endure as he had endured.

Touch the Sky had made up his mind and there was no going back. Ladislaw had already told him it took the better part of a day for the medicine to work—if it was going to. But Touch the Sky knew it was far too late to simply sit back and pray for a miracle from the white man's God.

No. He was his tribe's shaman. Arrow Keeper was no longer here to tell him what to do. It was up to him to act, to do something that might add strength to the white-skin medicine. And only one thing could help this late in the tragedy: an agonizing vigil of suffering as an offering to the high holy ones.

He stopped at Little Horse's tipi and roused his tired companion without waking Ladislaw, who slept on the other side of the center pole. "Come, buck," Touch the Sky said. "Shake out the cobwebs and wake to the living day. I need your assistance. I am going to set up a pole."

Little Horse knew his friend well and had been dreading something like this. Once before, up north in the Bear Paw Mountains, Touch the Sky had undergone self-inflicted torture to strengthen a prayer. That time, he had persuaded Little Horse to heap rocks onto his back until he was nearly crushed to death. But his suffering had induced the rare and powerful Indian magic known as the Iron Shirt—bluecoat bullets turned into sand and failed to kill even one member of Shoots Left Handed's beleagured Cheyenne band. But this disease seemed even more hopeless.

"Brother," Little Horse said, "you have done more than ten braves could have to save our people. But we were too late. You have suffered too much on this hard mission. Setting up a pole now could kill you."

"It could, buck. But so could the alternative."

Little Horse understood his meaning. His friend was telling him that, if Honey Eater crossed over, life would mean nothing to Touch the Sky. Reluctant, but knowing protest was useless, Little Horse followed his companion to a copse near the river. Touch the Sky selected a strong cottonwood limb and cut it free with his ax. He filed one end to a point while Little Horse reported to the lodge of the Bow String Troopers.

He returned with a crude leather harness, which was designed to be cinched over one end of the pole. Detachable metal hooks dangled from the harness. They fixed the harness to the pole, and Touch the Sky carried it to a small rise overlooking the entire camp. There, in the blazing midday sun, he dug a hole and lowered his penance pole into it.

"Drive the hooks in, brother," he said, "and don't be squeamish."

Wincing, trying to be quick and careful, Little Horse gouged two hooks into the muscles of Touch the Sky's chest. He had been sure to push the point between the cords of muscle, not through them, so there was not much blood. But the pain made Touch the Sky suck his breath in through his teeth.

"Now hook me up." He said with a gasp.

A few moments later, he dangled a few hand breadths above the ground—all his weight suspended from the hooks in his chest. For the rest of that day, while Sister Sun beat down on him mercilessly, Touch the Sky dangled in a welter of sweat, blood, and pain. Like a man riding through patchy fog, he drifted in and out of consciousness. Each time he surfaced to awareness, he saw Little Horse, Two Twists, and Tangle Hair gathered faithfully at the base of his pole. Despite their deep sympathy for his pain, however, not one of them lifted his hand to comfort Touch the Sky. Such a gesture could ruin the voluntary penance.

At first, only his loyal band had gathered. But soon Chief Gray Thunder heard of this sacrifice and came out to join them in silent camaraderie. As the day progressed, more and more of the people joined the group around his pole. Despite her deep pessimism, Sharp Nosed Woman had been struck by the tall brave's noble gesture. After all, where was Black Elk while his wife lay dying? Thus reasoning, she overcame her exhaustion and led the people in a spirited prayer to Maiyun.

Little Horse had taken Ladislaw to briefly meet Chief Gray Thunder before leading him to his own tipi for sleep. Now the wide-eyed white man stood at the bottom of the rise. He stared at Touch the Sky and at the growing ring of people. These Indians knew he was trying to help. But most either ignored him or treated him with cool civility, some were openly hostile.

Little Horse rose and gazed west toward the Wolf Mountains. Touch the Sky had said to bring him down when the sun's belly touched the peaks. The tall brave was conscious, but only barely.

Little Horse nodded at Tangle Hair and Two Twists. Then he gazed toward the pest lodge, dreading what was about to happen. Already, Ladislaw was slowly heading that way to check on the victims, who were probably cold corpses by now.

Little Horse knew that Touch the Sky had faced down every danger known to a warrior. But as was true with all brave, strong men, the wells of feeling in him, though silent, ran deep. What bullets and arrows and torture could not accomplish, the death of Honey Eater might achieve: the end of Touch the Sky too.

"Lift him," Little Horse told his friends, "but gently. I fear he must now face what the Wendigo himself would flee from."

Chapter Fifteen

For some time Touch the Sky lay in the cool grass where his friends had placed him. The pain in his chest muscles had long since sent roots and branches throughout the rest of his body.

He opened his eyes. Wincing at the sharp lance points of pain, he sat up; then, wobbling, he stood. Through all this, his sympathetic friends nonetheless refused to help him. There was no shame in requiring help, but it would have insulted him to offer it before he requested it. It was important for Touch the Sky to show the tribe that he did not need it now.

He looked at Little Horse, Two Twists, and Tangle Hair. Beyond them stood Chief Gray Thunder and Spotted Tail, leader of the Bow String Soldiers. Beyond them were the members of the tribe, except for his worst enemies, and any of the Bull Whip Soldiers. These last, following the instructions of their leader, Lone Bear, remained near Medicine Flute's tipi.

No more avoiding it, Touch the Sky knew. So much easier to face the awesome trick rider Comanche Big Tree, who could launch ten arrows before the first one struck its target; the mad renegade Blackfoot Sis-ki-dee, who killed a whiteskin infant by braining it against a tree in front of its mother; or even the Cherokee policeman Mankiller, whose huge and powerful hands could snap a man's neck like a dry sotol stalk.

How much harder to face the fact of seeing Honey Eater with no life in her. There were no muscles to tense for this blow, the one soft place in him that could become a hurting place for life.

"Where is the white-skin shaman?" Touch the Sky finally asked Little Horse.

"Brother, he went into the pest lodge some time ago. He has yet to emerge."

Touch the Sky fought back waves of dizziness and darker waves of pain from the badly abused muscles of his chest. He stared across the clearing at the hide-draped lodge. Then he nodded. His face wincing again at the incredible, fiery pain, he set off across the clearing.

Each step shot a jolting agony of pain through him. His friends followed close behind; then came Gray Thunder, Spotted Tail, and the rest of the people. There was an eerie, ceremonial importance to all of it that humbled everyone, even Touch the Sky's harshest critics.

Little Horse was given to making morbid jokes to help his comrades ease their battle fear. But he understood that such comments would be as wrong as small talk during the Renewal Prayer. He felt he was seeing something more important than the daily suffering—the elemental, powerful holiness of a right and pure and strong love.

Two Twists openly let a tear course down his cheek, and the defiant scowl that accompanied it dared any man to call him a woman for it. Not only was his favorite uncle inside that lodge, probably dead, but he was Honey Eater's closest friend besides Touch the Sky. Often had he risked his life from Black Elk's wrath to slip her a comforting word about Touch the Sky.

Touch the Sky was perhaps a stone's throw away from the lodge when the entrance flap was thrown back and Dr. Ladislaw emerged. The white man's eyes met the red man's. His face looked like that of a man suddenly waking up in a strange room in a strange town. Touch the Sky couldn't quite read that expression. But he felt a cold rock replace his stomach when he saw Ladislaw shake his head in what could only signify a gesture of final defeat.

Touch the Sky spoke in English. "Is it over?"

The contract surgeon stepped aside. He stared out over the serrated peaks of the mountains, as if he had a feeble brain awed by his first view of the West. "Can't be," he muttered.

"Did you hear me?" Touch the Sky demanded.

Ladislaw clearly heard nothing at that moment, except some secret and private music in the spheres. He stared at Touch the Sky. "You know, I promised myself that if God ever showed Himself to me once, even just once, I'd quit my sinning. Well, He called my hand today!"

The contract surgeon's distraught face and odd mutterings had sent some of the people nervously backing away. Clearly, the sight of all the death had unnerved him, many thought.

"Ladislaw!" Touch the Sky snapped. "To hell with your chatter. How are they?"

"Go see for yourself," Ladislaw replied, stepping farther aside.

It was only a few steps, but the longest walk of Touch the Sky's life. His legs hung back like stone weights, so reluctant was he to look inside that lodge and face perhaps the cruelest fact of his fate. Blood still oozed from the punctures in his chest as he finished crossing to the pest lodge.

Again Ladislaw shook his head. "There's only one word for it," he said quietly, even as Touch the Sky steeled himself to look inside. "Miracle."

Touch the Sky heard the word just as his eyes found Honey Eater's. Hers were open. And even from there, he could see the weak but clear glint of vitality in those eyes!

"Tall warrior," she said, her voice faint but recognizable, "Sharp Nosed Woman says we all owe you our lives—once again. As always, I see from looking at you that you have paid dearly for sending death away."

Not just Honey Eater—all were recovering. Trains the Hawk, Two Twists' uncle, mustered a weak smile. Even little Laughing Brook, though not yet living up to her name, smiled weakly at the handsome young warrior.

"A miracle," Ladislaw said again. "They were gone. I only administered that medicine to humor you."

The people outside the lodge were abuzz with exclamations and praise as the words flew through camp: The sick ones were healed! White man's medicine had combined with red man's medicine, and the sick ones were recovering!

An exultant cry of praise was lifted to Maiyun. The camp crier leapt on his pony and tore through the village streets, announcing this miracle to the rest. Excited word bringers were sent to bring the good news to the far-flung Cheyenne bands.

"Touch the Sky," Gray Thunder said, "your acts during council, when you seized the voting stones, amounted to treason. But as I told you then, the act would be vindicated by success. Soon, thanks to you, our distant clans will join us for the feasting and celebrations. We will never forget those we have lost to this terrible disease. But better to dwell on the number who were saved."

His eyes flicked from Touch the Sky to each of the braves who had ridden with him—and to the white-skin doctor who, in spite of his obvious fear, used his skill to save suffering Indians.

"Arrow Keeper spoke the straight word," Gray Thunder told Touch the Sky, "When he said your path would be a violent and bloody one. Trouble comes looking for you like a bear grubbing for beetles. But I will never forget what that wise old shaman also said. You are a taller man by far than the tallest, and you have the true and rare gift of the vision seeker. More trouble is coming, surely. But in you, buck, trouble has met a worthy foe!"

Despite Gray Thunder's public vote of confidence, Touch the Sky and many others did not miss his reference to more trouble coming. Indeed, the main source of all future trouble returned to camp the very next day—or rather limped into camp.

Touch the Sky was still resting in his tipi when he heard a ripple of scornful laughter flying through the camp. He also heard taunting jeers. He rose, stiff with pain, and lifted the elkskin flap of his tipi. At first he saw nothing unusual. Then he spotted Black Elk, Wolf Who Hunts Smiling, and Swift Canoe. Surely it was the most humiliating moment of their lives. For all three rode old, swayback mules obviously stolen from some white-skin corral or mining camp.

"Returned are the mighty heroes!" someone shouted. "They have swapped their ponies for fine mules with mange!"

Death Camp

"Look! Here is Black Elk, one day after his squaw is saved! Too bad he was not here to see it!"

Touch the Sky could not help a wide smile at the ridiculous sight these three braggarts presented. Wolf Who Hunts Smiling looked especially ludicrous. His mule's back swayed so deep it left the Cheyenne's moccasins dragging on the ground. This, plus the brave's deep scowl, sent some warriors to the ground in laughing fits.

The entire camp had crowded into the clearing, laughing, staring, pointing. His face furious with rage, Wolf Who Hunts Smiling stopped in the middle of camp. As if defiantly, he refused to get off the mule.

"Cheyenne people! Have ears for my words!" His eyes found Touch the Sky's as he spoke. "Enjoy your mirth! Well do I and certain others note the faces of those traitors to the Cheyenne way who mock us now. The simple brains among you have not yet seen the truth. A war is coming and soon! Not a war with bluecoats or Pawnee or Crow—a war within the Cheyenne tribe!"

His words were sobering. Now no one laughed. "Those who mock my cousin and me, look closer. Look over by Medicine Flute's tent. Count the Bull Whips gathered over there. Count their scalps. You who mock are many in number. But many of you are elders or women. Those gathered over by that tipi are warriors in their prime. They do not

173

laugh at pretend Indians who secretly play the dog for white-skins!"

Wolf Who Hunts Smiling had always been a commanding speaker, and he was in his prime now. He continued to stare at Touch the Sky, murder clear in his eyes.

"You call this one your shaman and let him keep our sacred arrows. He who defied his chief openly in council, who went over the entire Council of Forty. I tell you this: From where I stand now to the sun's resting place there is no spot for this one to hide from my wrath! I will kill this false shaman! And many more will die with him if they are foolish enough to follow him."

In a flash, Wolf Who Hunts Smiling had drawn back his arm and let his lance fly. Only at the last moment did Touch the Sky move his head in time. The lance missed his throat by mere inches and struck the cottonwood beside his tipi.

Wolf Who Hunts Smiling threw back his head and laughed. The tribe was silent as they watched the three new arrivals cross to join their Bull Whip brothers. For a moment, before he went back inside his tipi, Touch the Sky's eyes lifted across toward the tipi where Honey Eater was resting, getting her strength back.

Wolf Who Hunts Smiling was right, he thought. A war was coming, and many would die. Just as Arrow Keeper had told Touch the Sky, just as his vision at Medicine Lake had confirmed. The battle lines were clearly drawn; the sides marked out.

Death Camp

Once the war cry sounded, the holy ones must have mercy on his enemies, for Touch the Sky would not.

"Wolf Who Hunts Smiling!"

The voice startled everyone. Wolf Who Hunts Smiling turned, as did everyone else, to stare at young Two Twists. He stood next to Little Horse and Tangle Hair.

Contempt starched into every feature, Two Twists lifted his clout—a gesture of mocking derision clearly reserved for outright enemies of the tribe.

Wolf Who Hunts Smiling's rage was instant. But Little Horse's raised shotgun persuaded him to leave his Colt in its sheath. So angered was Wolf Who Hunts Smiling that he could not immediately speak. Medicine Flute, ever loyal to his master, hurried forward.

"Many call themselves shamen," he shouted in the voice that had never quite lost its adolescent tendency to break on the high notes. "But any man can put the trance glaze over his eyes and pretend to visions. I say only this. Wolf Who Hunts Smiling has spoken straight arrow. The importance of his words will soon be confirmed in a sign."

Before Touch the Sky could worry what new treachery this prediction meant, Wolf Who Hunts Smiling's mule made it come true. It suddenly lifted its tail and left a huge pile of droppings in the middle of the camp. The roar of laughter throughout camp was instantaneous.

But as he dropped the flap of his tipi again, a smile still dividing his face, Touch the Sky could not help again hearing the words of old Arrow Keeper: *Laughter, while necessary, always gives way to tears.*